An Odyssey

An Odyssey

Hiking The Bruce Trail

Lorraine McLennan

Library of Congress Control Number:		2012907248
ISBN:	Hardcover	978-1-4771-0104-9
	Softcover	978-1-4771-0103-2
	Ebook	978-1-4771-0105-6

This book describes the author's experiences while hiking with three friends on the Bruce Trail and reflects her opinions relating to those experiences. All names, and incidents are true. The distances hiked are approximate due to detours, and route changes made over the years. We did however hike the entire trail from Queenston, Ontario to Tobermory, Ontario.

This book was printed in the United States of America.

To order additional copies of this book, contact:
Xlibris Corporation
1-888-795-4274
www.Xlibris.com
Orders@Xlibris.com
103018

Contents

DEDICATION

To Ric, my husband, for his constant encouragement

To Heather, Carrie, Cole and Jennifer my
Beloved family for whom this was written.

To Mary and Bernice my adventure companions.

With love to all.

An odyssey, according to *Webster's Dictionary*, is a series of wanderings and adventures. In starting to hike the Bruce Trail, we didn't intend to "wander," but we were hoping for an "adventure."

Staying strictly on the trail was interesting, informative, invigorating, and exhausting. However, wandering off the trail into places unknown became the wonderful adventures that we experienced. Initially we had no idea what we were getting into but reflections now at the end of this, our great odyssey, we are thrilled and happy to have had these experiences.

Our names are Bernice Scott, Mary Oberholtzer, and Lorraine McLennan.

Our plan is to walk the Bruce Trail from Niagara Falls on to Tobermory, Ontario.

Our hope is to complete the trail in five years.

Our prayer is to keep healthy enough to finish it.

As three friends from grade school, we got together regularly through the years to remember the past, enjoy the present, and contemplate the future.

As for the past, Mary always says we grew up in the best of times. Of course it was the war years, the forties; and during that period, many things became part of our lives. We had food rationing, and so often, foods such as sugar, flour, butter, and meat were bought with food stamps that were given out by the government. The stamps were often traded with friends and other family members if the need for certain ingredients arose—for example, if one needed extra flour or sugar for a birthday cake or for cookies to send overseas to friends and family.

Gas too was rationed, which made walking a necessity for everyone. In fact, cars were scarce; and if you were lucky enough to own one, you had to keep it because cars were not manufactured between 1941 and 1945 due to the *war effort*. This term was familiar to many at the time because the whole country was prepared for the supply and demand of war supplies.

As children in school, we were very patriotic, singing songs of love for kin and country and saving our pennies for Red Cross Day, which was every Friday afternoon. These pennies went to buy bandages and other medical supplies and wool to knit scarves, socks, etc., for the soldiers overseas. With so many men away at war, women were taking over jobs in factories and stores, filling in whenever possible.

In fact, for us, it was a great time. Our small town of Preston had a lovely swimming pool and a full-sized arena, a beautiful park by the Nith River, and a pretty little park in the uptown area with a cenotaph from the First World War. And next to the park, we had our Park Theatre. We spent some Saturday afternoons at shows, watching the latest movie, a serial, and a cartoon—all for 12¢ per person.

All summer long, we spent mornings having swimming lessons and afternoons perfecting those lessons and lazing around the park before and after the swimming times passed.

In the winter, we went ice-skating at the arena every Saturday afternoon and tried to be another Barbara Ann Scott, Canada's 1948 Olympic gold medalist. Needless to say, we usually ended up sitting on the ice while trying the various twists and turns of a professional figure skater. Even so, it was fun, and we skated every chance we had. The streets were covered in ice from December to the end of March. In our small town, we would sometimes just skate around the streets in the neighborhood.

As the years passed, we continued to get together, and it was on one such occasion that someone suggested we do something exciting and try hiking the Bruce Trail from beginning to end. We all spent many hours in the outdoors growing up. Going on little hikes, both by foot and by bike, was a pastime we had often enjoyed. So began our plans to hike the Bruce. At the median age of sixty-seven, we felt we had better begin sooner than later. Thus, on Thursday, August 9, 2001, we began our Bruce Trail odyssey. This book is a recollection of those adventures.

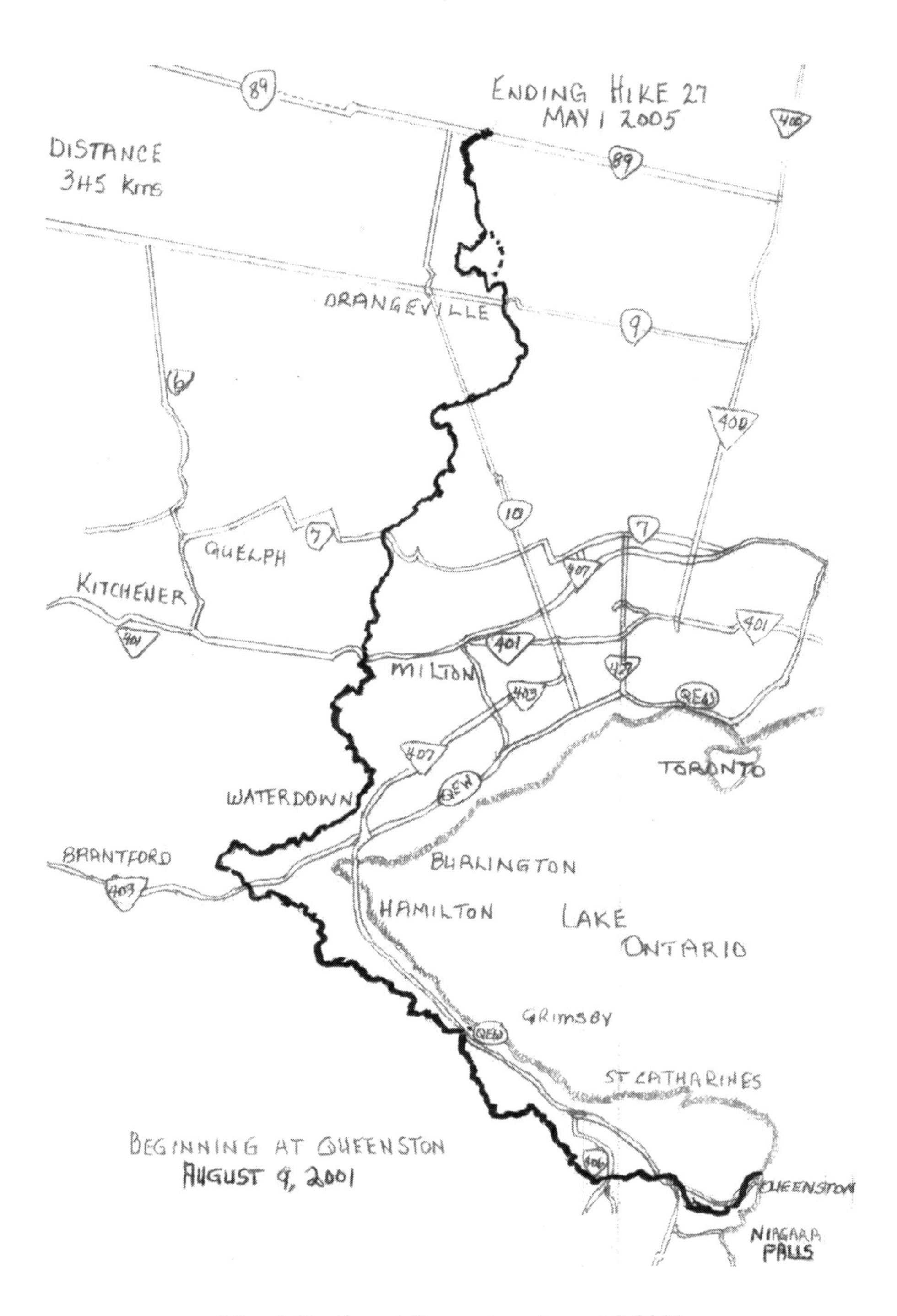

Map 1 Starting at Queenston, August 9 2001

Hike No. 1

August 9, 2001

We began our very first hike on August 9, 2001, at 7:52 a.m., at the Bruce Trail cairn at Queenston, Ontario, Canada, on one of the hottest days of 2001.

Close up of plaque at Cairn Queenston Hike #1 2001 The temperature at 7:00 a.m. was 27°C (80°F). <

The Beginning Lorraine Mary Bernice August 9 2001

When we began, we were in the shade of the beautiful trees of Queenston Heights Park, and we were quite comfortable. However, as we continued, our body temperatures increased; and before long, we were really feeling the heat. We soon learned that hiking in above 25° C weather was just not what we wanted to do and had an impact on our decisions for all our hikes in the future.

It was exciting for us to begin our plan to walk the entire trail. At the average ages of sixty-seven, it was a lofty idea. We had all been walking almost every day for about an hour a day and were, fortunately, all in good health; but hiking the roads and paths of our neighborhoods was nothing compared with what we would encounter on the trail.

The walk was exhilarating, exciting, and interesting; and the scenery was simply beautiful. The trail was wide in most areas, well marked, and not difficult. We crossed a fast-moving stream within the first half hour. The area was mostly, filled with lofty maples, willows and other deciduous trees, grapevines, of course, the rocky cliffs of the peninsula. We reached St. Davids, Ontario, and continued through to Fireman's Park, an area so named because the local firemen maintain the park. It is a very hilly area, with a pond with fish, frogs, and other pond life. We continued coming in from the back of the park, up the hill to the main park entrance, arriving at 10:28 a.m. The temperature now was 32°C or 90°F. The distance was 6.8 km.

We felt fine, other than being very warm. We had rested three times and consumed two bottles of water each and light snacks of crackers and apples. We would have loved to continue our walk, if not for the extreme heat; and as the next lap was mostly in the open with the sun directly overhead, we decided we would wait to continue on a cooler day.

Since my husband, Ric, had dropped us off at the cairn in Queenston, I phoned him requesting for a ride home.

Ric at Cairn Hike #1 2001

He picked us up. Arriving back at our house, to say we were happy with our beginning was an understatement. We were thrilled and eager to do the next lap in about a month, when the climate would be cooler. And so the adventure began . . .

Hike No. 2

September 21, 2001

We continued our second hike from the lower parking area of Fireman's Park, Friday, September 21, 2001, where we had left off on our first hike. It was a good hiking day, with the temperature in the mid seventies, a big improvement over the last time.

We began hiking around the northern side of the pond and almost immediately began to climb back into the woods. Our newly purchased walking sticks (custom-made by a gentleman in Cambridge, Ontario) turned out to be a definite asset as we climbed a steep hill, leaving the pond area behind. We were thankful to have these walking sticks in many, many occasions in the future.

We followed a well-marked, well-kept trail through a treed area to Mewburn Road, past a trailer park, crossing over railway tracks, and over the Queen Elizabeth Highway and through fields that eventually led us to Woodend Conservation Area. We hiked along the brow of the escarpment, and below us was the Niagara on Lake Campus of Niagara College, the Skyway Bridge crossing over the Welland Canal, and some vineyards—a very important industry of the Niagara Region. We had a lovely view of the Toronto Ontario, skyline from across Lake Ontario.

As we hiked, darkening skies hurried us along, as we did not want to get caught in a thunderstorm. We passed a nursery and some lovely country homes, and it eventually led us to the farther end of Woodend

Conservation Area. We decided to end our second leg of the trail at this point, and Ric came again to pick us up and return us to Mary's car, which was parked back at Fireman's Park. We had completed approximately 15.8 km in our first two hikes.

Hike No. 3

November 17, 2001

We were delayed from hiking until Saturday, November 17· With Canadian Thanksgiving, many family birthday celebrations, and early Christmas shopping keeping us all busy, it was the earliest date we were able to get together.

We had agreed our meeting place for this hike would be the Mohawk Access Trail parking area on Hamilton Mountain, overlooking the city of Hamilton, and again with a great view of Lake Ontario. It was the halfway point for Bernice and Mary coming from Cambridge and me coming from Niagara Falls. It was a bright sunny day, a little nippy in the shaded areas, a temperature of 12-14°C. (56-58°F.), but we were enjoying being out in the fresh air. We had also chosen this section, assuming we would probably just hike along the brow of the mountain and end up at the finishing point of Mountain Brow Boulevard. Never assume! We started with a long walk on a paved walkway down to the bottom of the mountain, along about 1 km (0.6 miles) and arrived at a very long flight of stairs back up the mountain. This method of hiking the mountain brow continued, first up and then down, but always with a beautiful view of the city (from the top). We lost track of the number of times this occurred, and it surely wasn't what we expected! We had a good laugh over it anyway and commented on how lucky we were to be able to enjoy the beautiful day, the view, and the hike. As we arrived at the Sherman Access Road leading back to the top of the escarpment, we stopped for a lunch break and to view once again the Toronto skyline.

As we reached the parking area, a group of people were paragliding off the side of the mountain. It sure looked exciting, but we believed we were quite comfortable just to have our feet on the ground. We had covered 11.8 km (7.32 miles) on this day and a total of approximately 30 km for the first year of our Odyssey. We realized it was a long, long distance stretching out in front of us. We were determined and looking forward to the spring of 2002, wondering where and when we would meet again for our hike no. 4.

Hike No. 4

April 30, 2002

After the long winter, we began our 2002 hiking year on April 30 at 10:15 a.m. at Woodend near St. Catharines, Ontario. The day dawned gray and rainy, and my first inclination was to call Bernice and Mary to cancel. Instead, I switched on the local weather channel, which only confirmed my first thought was probably the right one. However, having cancelled once already this New Year, I really couldn't have faced Bernice if the weather cleared later on, so I prepared as per my plan and met with Bernice and Mary at the pre-appointed place at the Pen Centre, St. Catharines. Leaving Mary's car there, we drove to Woodend to begin.

Fortunately, the rain had stopped by this time, but cloud cover remained. Being the hearty souls that we were (determined too), we started out with backpacks, the usual light snacks, and a throwaway camera. Mary, our official photographer, decided this was a good idea in case the pictures were so bad that we could throw the camera away in a mad fit, as it is always the fault of the camera if the pictures didn't turn out.

In the spring, a young man's fancy turns to thoughts of love, and hiking trails turn to ruts of mud, which in turn adheres to your boots. Needless to say, with the mud and the added weight of our boots, we were happy to have our walking sticks with us, which were invaluable to help us on our way. Although underfoot was sloppy and slippery, we were careful to watch where we stepped. Once again, the scenery caught us off guard.

Beyond the well-traveled roads of the area is the history of an era in its quiet repose. The very first Welland Canal was part of that scene, hidden by brush and overgrowth and quietly reminding one of a much earlier time. Huge rocks cut from the local rock to form the walls of the canal were amazing. Stone overpasses beginning to break away and an old steel bridge standing silent in a now wasteland is a monument to a previous era.

Old Steel Railroad Bridge Old Welland Canal Hike No 4 2002

The First Welland Canal was built in 1829, with rebuilds in 1845, 1887, and 1932. The canal crosses the Niagara Peninsula from Lake Erie to Lake Ontario, with seven lift locks to raise and lower the ships passing through. It is interesting to see these huge oceangoing vessels being lifted simply by forcing more water into the lock. The vessels continue through the lakes, down the St. Lawrence River to the Atlantic Ocean, which is a marvelous navigational feat.

As we continued, a jolt brought us back to the present as we exited out of the woods to a path that skirted a beautiful, lush, green golf course. Today's world rejoined!

Following along the canal, we arrived at Glendale Avenue, past the General Motors automotive manufacturing plant and crossed over the bridge of the present Welland Canal. We stopped here for our healthy light snack and a well-deserved rest at around 12:30 p.m. By now the sun was shining down on our ambitious outing, and a light breeze was blowing, keeping us very comfortable in our enjoyable walk.

After ascending a slight incline, we came to a small cement bridge and along some old canal sections. Going down about twelve steps and passing through an area that looked like the side of an old stone overpass, we encountered five or six teenage boys hanging around. Lots of graffiti on the walls of the bridge made us feel like we were entering some private teenage club, but the boys were friendly, taking their school lunch break, and they assured us we were on the right track to our destination. We made our way to Glendale Avenue and on to Mary's car. We discarded our muddy boots, poles, and backpacks, etc., into Mary's trunk and drove to my car at Woodend, arriving at 3:45 p.m. From there we drove to my house for a celebratory drink and dinner and were a much less tired troupe than we were previously. The trek was again much shorter than we had hoped, only approximately 10.5 km, so next time a longer trip will have to be planned.

Bernice and Mary left for home around 6:10 p.m., and I hoped they enjoyed the day as much as I did!

Hike No. 5

June 2, 2002

This trek started out on a beautiful Sunday morning, June 2, 2002, with our meeting at The Log Cabin Restaurant in Fonthill, Ontario. Bernice and Mary followed me to the ending base where we transferred the appropriate items from one car to the other and then drove on to the Pen Centre, where we had left off on our last hike.

We left the Pen Centre and headed up a hill to a wooded area and then through a woodsy and grassy area and past some very interesting carvings. One carving was of a mother bear and two cubs and there were also some carvings that, at first glance, looked like a skull looking over a fallen log. Upon closer view it turned out to be a rock, and it was painted and shaped (either by nature or by hand) just like a skull.

Skull on trail Hike #5 2002

This walk followed a footpath on the Brock University Campus. Brock has a large campus, and a variety of courses are offered. We continued along a fence at the top of the escarpment and some rather scrubby land that brought us to Lake Moodie. We left the trail and walked a short way and stopped for our lunch break on the banks of the very lovely lake. We teased Mary as she stopped to retouch her make up or perhaps apply some sun shade. We decided it was the latter.

Mary @ Lake Moodie Hike #5 2002

Bernice and I at Lake Moodie Hike #5 2002

We continued around the lake, and at the other side we came to DeCew Falls. It is another of the many beautiful waterfalls in the Niagara Region. We headed up past DeCew Falls and some beautiful country homes and then turned left again into a wooded area. This took us across a creek and along some low lands and brush areas, again crossing some water beds, and eventually up a rather steep hill to a gravel road on the edge of Shorthills Provincial Park. The park is home to coyotes and white-tailed deer too! However, we didn't encounter any on our walk through their home areas. Horseback riding, mountain biking, and fishing are all activities enjoyed there. We arrived at our car at 3:45 p.m. It had been a good walk, the weather was great for hiking, and we felt pretty good.

We drove to the Pen Centre to get something to eat before we headed back home. While we indulged ourselves with food, we planned our next outing for either Tuesday, June 11, or Thursday, the thirteenth. I thought we were definitely getting better at this and were ready for the next leg as soon as we could make arrangements within our time tables and with the weatherman. This trip was 14.2 km, making our total to date of 52.3 km or approximately 33 miles. The trail is long, but the hikes are short in distance; and with determination and "a little bit of luck, a little bit of luck, with a little bit of blooming luck" (a song from *My Fair Lady*), we will "suck it up" and "git 'er dun." (This became our favorite phrase and was to be repeated many, many times!)

Hike No. 6

June 13, 2002

Our third hike of 2002 began on Thursday, June 13, and we met on a lovely morning at the junction of Highway 81, west of St. Catharines. I arrived first and was engrossed in the maps spread out over the trunk of my car when Mary and Bernice arrived. We had to ascertain where we were going to park the other car so as not to make the hike too long, but also not too short either. There was not always a place to park the car at the destination we would like to hike back to. So after scouting the area, we arrived at a parking area at Pelham Road and left Mary's car there and proceeded back to our starting point.

It was just about 10:00 a.m. when we started down the gravel road along a fence line looking over Short Hills Provincial Park. What a great view! We came to a series of horse farms, which we skirted, walking through some long grasses wet from the previous night's rain. Soon we were just as wet as the grasses, as the trail had not yet been cleared of the long grass. We arrived at a steep ascent to the top of the escarpment, where we finally emerged by the Rockway Community Centre, at Fifteen Mile Creek. Lunching at the picnic tables were several young people who had also been hiking. Some others were rock climbing where the waterfall drops over the steep cliffs.

We walked along the road for a short way and into another very mature wooded area, very peaceful and quiet, and we rested on a large fallen log. At our feet, a carpet of fallen leaves circled a campfire pit. Evidently, others had chosen the fallen log as a resting place too. After a very steep incline and a gradual decline and over a stream and a swampy area, we came upon another lovely little waterfall. It was quite the view with the afternoon sun filtering through the trees and glinting off the water. Mary snapped a few photos as we climbed over some huge rocks, no doubt pushed and shoved into place by the last glacier and ice age. We soon exited to our parking area and drove back to pick up my car. We traded our "hikers" for normal footwear, spruced up our hairdos and makeup, and drove to Fonthill, Ontario to the Log Cabin Restaurant again for a very tasty early dinner. We had completed our 12-km hike by 4:00 p.m. but decided we must lengthen our hikes if we intend to finish this trail in our lifetime.

Hike No. 7

September 4, 2002

We chose Wednesday, September 4, for our fourth hike of 2002, where we had left off on our last hike. At 10:10 a.m. it was another beautiful day, and it encouraged us to step right out with a feeling of a great hike ahead. (Little did we know . . .)

We hiked past Staff Farm and then turned north on 17 St. Louth for quite a way and then west into the woods, climbing up the escarpment to 21 Louth. We arrived at Balls Falls Conservation Area around 12:30 p.m., a distance of approximately 5.1 km. These falls are beautiful and approximately two-thirds the size of Niagara Falls, making them a sight to see. Having been to Balls Falls myself several times in the past, I rather took over as tour guide. We perused the old pioneer buildings and learned there had been a grist mill, saw mill, and woolen mills there when it was founded in the early nineteenth century and are open to the public in the summertime. We walked over to the brink of the falls and were very surprised to see the falls completely dry, as Twelve Mile Creek can dry up with no water cascading over the brink at all during a long hot summer. It had been a very hot summer.

With all of our wandering around, we missed the blaze and walked up the road quite a distance before realizing our mistake and headed back into the wooded area high above the riverbed. Not much to be said for my qualities as a tour guide! We stopped for lunch and rested, as we were tiring from the heat. It had seemed to be a difficult hike thus far, but the best (or worst) was yet to come.

We came to a large area of trees. Again the blazes were few and badly marked. Forging on, we came to the edge of the escarpment overlooking fields and grape vineyards, of which there are many in the Niagara area. We continued into a very rocky area, along the escarpment edge, and by now it was nearly 4:00 p.m. We were becoming uneasy with the terrain and the heavily treed area, and we didn't seem to be heading in the direction we thought we should be going. As evening sets in early at this time of year, we didn't want to get caught in the woods in the dark. We turned back and fortunately came upon two hikers who directed us to an old lumber trail, which led directly to a farmer's property. This was the junction of Moyer Road and Spiece Road. By now it was 5:45 p.m., and we were really tired.

We knocked on the door of the farmer's house and his wife answered, and she said he was just coming down the road with the tractor. He parked his tractor for the night and kindly offered to drive us to our car, which was on Quarry Road, a five-minute drive by car but at least an hour by foot through the bush. We were so grateful for the ride and thanked the farmer for assisting the damsels in distress.

We collapsed into the car and rested for a while and then drove to Beamsville for a well-deserved dinner. It was now 6:30 p.m., and as we were long overdue for our usual time, I called Ric, my husband, to assure him we were safe and sound, albeit hungry, and it would still be sometime before we officially ended our day.

We accomplished 15.8 km and decided to be more cautious when planning our future hikes. This was becoming quite a learning experience. I had always liked learning on the job! I am not sure Bernice and Mary agreed with me, and we didn't realize then how much of a learning experience this would become. Hiking didn't seem to require a whole lot of knowledge, as far as we were concerned. We obviously didn't have a whole lot when it came to hiking. But we did learn, oh yes.

Hike No. 8

September 15,2002

On September 15, we began our fifth hike of 2002 on an overcast Sunday morning. We decided to meet at the Regional Niagara Headquarters at Bartlett and Central Avenue just off the Queen Elizabeth Way at Exit 68. As you may realize, most of these areas are unfamiliar to us, so much of our time is taken up just allocating parking places, as I have said before.

There was no parking area, so I headed up to the next intersection and turned around to park in a nursing home parking lot on Central Avenue. Bernice and Mary arrived at almost the same time, 9:00 a.m., but turned up at Central. They, meanwhile, were sitting farther up the street, waiting and watching for me. Eventually, Mary walked down to Bartlett, and we spied one another. We began to wonder—if we couldn't find each other on the highways and byways of suburbia, how could we expect to find our way in the hills and fields of the Bruce Trail.

Finding our way to Ridge Road East, we left one car at what would be our finishing place and drove back to the infamous Quarry Road (the area of our previous wandering) to start hike no. 5 of 2002. It was our eighth hike in all.

The sky was overcast at 9:30 a.m. and the air fairly cool. We headed into the bush and came upon a deep gully. The decline is through rocks and is called Jacob's Ladder. It was a little touchy to get through. We then carried on to Kinsman Community Park. The trail was very well marked, and we didn't miss any blazes this time and continued on to

Mountainview Road, where we stopped for our lunch. Power Bars are great for rejuvenation, and after a few minutes of rest we started up another steep climb, crossing many dried-up gullies and arriving at Thirty Mile Road.

We met a couple of young fellows on dirt bikes contemplating riding through the trail. We advised against it, having just completed it ourselves and believing the terrain a little difficult for bike riding. We crossed Mountainview Road and were back into the woods in no time. We arrived at our destination and had completed our 10.3 km. We headed back to Beamsville for a quick snack and a bit of a rest and were happy we completed our walk in such good time. Bidding farewell till the next time, we headed off in opposite directions for home.

Hike No. 9

October 26, 2002

It had been some time since our last hike. Unfortunately, Mary wasn't feeling too well and had put off hiking, hoping to improve. After tests, the results made it necessary for Mary to discontinue hiking with us. We were disappointed, as was Mary, but our health was the most important factor in accomplishing this task and had to be taken seriously. However, she decided to assist us in our quest and agreed to meet us at the end of our hikes so that we could begin without having to find someplace to park the other car at the end of the hike each time, which saved us much time. So on Saturday, October 26, Bernice and I met at Grimsby for our ninth hike. We made a quick pit stop at Tim Horton's before beginning another day on the trail.

Leaving home, it was foggy and had rained in the night, so we rather anticipated a very damp walk. Although it was somewhat muddy underfoot and rather slippery because of the fallen leaves on the rocks, it didn't rain. The temperature was 4-5°C (40°F), very comfortable for a day's hiking.

This hike turned out to be one of better ones, trail wise, as it was well kept, well marked, and not too difficult. We phoned Mary to make sure we were going to rendezvous at the appointed place and time (3:00 p.m.). We came upon a strange-looking building. It was circular with a small door in the front, built on a semicircular foundation and into the side of the hill.) We never did find out what it was. We stopped around 12:15 p.m. for our lunch and a bit of a rest.

We headed west, descended over several streams, back up a steep climb to Mountain and Ridge roads. After hiking a few meters, we descended steeply back to Mountain Road and across a bridge at Forty Mile Creek and again back into the woods. At this point we had completed the Niagara section of the trail and began with the Iroquois Area.

This section was unbelievable. Most of the trail was wide enough for both of us to walk side by side, which was nice because, for some reason, I usually led the way and Bernice followed behind. The inclines (one of which took us from the bottom of the escarpment to the very top) were well maintained, wide, level, and with well-supported steps to aid in the climb. Bernice became our hike photographer and took a few pictures along the way.

One picture was of Old Grist Mill from 1795. Other shots were taken from Grimsby Point Bluff, which encompassed the escarpment to the right, with the Queen Elizabeth Way weaving its way to Niagara, and Lake Ontario to the left, with an array of fall colors.

View Looking Back at Niagara Hike 9 2002

This was part of the Beamers Conservation Area from which we soon exited to Ridge Road. From there we headed westward to Woolverton Mountain Road where we were to meet Mary. As we neared the corner, who should drive by but Mary who had also just arrived. It was 2:58 p.m. How's that for timing? We were glad to see Mary and were surprised at how well we had managed the trail. It was probably due to the cooler weather and the well-maintained trail.

Mary drove us to our cars, and from there we found a lovely little restaurant in Grimsby, where we had a sandwich and planned our next trek. We said our good-byes, pleased with our sixth hike of 2002. We had completed 13.km this time.

Hike No. 10

November 6, 2002

Hoping to have at least one, possibly two, walks in before year-end, we arranged for this date, Wednesday, November 6, 2002, with a backup date of November 10. The last two or three hikes, it had rained the night before and more was predicted for this day, but being the sturdy souls we are, we forged ahead and met at the Woolverton parking area a few minutes ahead of schedule—Bernice having taken the back way from Cambridge via the Lincoln Alexander Parkway, and I from my home down the Queen Elizabeth Way.

As Mary, once again, was prepared to be our pickup person, we had planned to phone her before we began just to clarify the details. However, neither of us could reach her, as we were out of cell phone range. We wondered what good they would be in the woods if we really needed to call for help. I, however, had my trusty Girl Guide whistle, which I had kept from my Girl Guide days and might have been some help if we had enough breath left to blow after hiking. We decided to update our cell phones, which was a wise decision on our part.

We started off at 9:07 a.m. with the sun breaking through (sometimes you just have to trust Mother Nature) and the weather a little cool at 3° C. With our headbands, mitts, and warm jackets, we went along Woolverton Mountain Road to the Winona conservation area and hiked along the brow of the escarpment with several lookout points. It reminded us of our hike last November when we had looked across the lake at the Toronto skyline. The trail was good except for wet fallen leaves, so we watched our steps. We encountered a couple of squirrels, and Bernice caught sight of a deer bounding through the trees. A flock of Canada geese were honking and cheering us on or maybe just announcing their departure to warmer climes.

Unfortunately, just before we tried to reach Mary on the phone again, with Bernice leading the expedition at this point, Bernice lost her footing and tumbled about ten feet down the not-too-steep hill, mostly sliding on her side. Thankfully, the only injuries were a couple of bruises on her leg. We breathed a sigh of relief, vowed to be even more careful, and carried on.

We continued to try to reach Mary for about two hours, and after gradually descending to the bottom of the escarpment, we realized we had been trying to get through the middle of a beautiful hard maple bush with trees towering over our heads interrupting any possible reception. Mary thought we had forgotten her or just couldn't reach her. However, we eventually contacted her, and we arranged to meet around 2:00 p.m. So far the trail had been great, and we were making really excellent time. So much for that! We will get into "that" later!

We trekked on for another half hour or so, and with the sun shining, a few fluffy white clouds, and a beautiful autumn day, we found a log situated with a good view of Lake Ontario and had our midday break and our usual snacks.

Starting out again at around 12:45 p.m., we realized that the "rugged terrain" described in the Bruce Trail Association trail reference meant exactly that. It was indeed very slow going because of the wet leaves on the slippery rocks and mud underfoot.

Believing we were treading very carefully didn't mean a thing, because, heading down a very slight decline, I took a header and landed face down and realized my hand and walking stick were underneath me. Again, there was no serious injury. However, my hand did feel some strain and swelled but was good as new within a couple of days. Again, you can't be too careful hiking in the bush!

As we were nearing the new subdivision and the end of our hike, we encountered a downed tree barring our path completely. We were halfway up a medium-sized hill on the edge of a wide gully and had to crawl under several smaller branches in order to continue and then edge along on our backs and sides until we could reach firmer ground. In another three quarters of an hour, we arrived at the MacDui Drive

Access Trail exit. No Mary, so we walked about a block to our east and back the other way to see if there was a parking area. The trail guide said there was roadside parking, so we walked back to the corner, and just then, we saw Mary coming down the street. Mary had also encountered a problem while looking for a Dewitt Drive. Upon finding it, she found out it was a one-way street going the other way. Finding an alternative route in a strange place took a few minutes. With all the mishaps, we managed to meet almost at 2:50 p.m.

We drove back to our cars, changed from our extremely muddy clothes and boots, and drove to the rest stop at Casablanca Boulevard and Queen Elizabeth Way, where we had a lovely dinner and updated each other with the latest news of the day. After another exciting, wonderful day, gratified and content, we headed home. Another 10.7 km were added to the distance.

Hike No. 11

November 24, 2002

Since Mary was again missing our outing, she promised to pick us up at the end of the day at the appointed place—the Mountain Brow Boulevard and Mohawk Access Trail parking lot. This is where we ended up on our last hike of 2001.

In Niagara, we had rain all day on Friday, and it turned to snow in the evening with an accumulation of about 3-5 inches. We had agreed if neither Bernice nor I heard from the other by 8:00 a.m. Sunday morning, we would start out. So early Sunday morning, November 24, Bernice and I met at MacDui Drive and started out promptly at 9:01 a.m. with temperatures at 3°C (40°F). Before long, the sun was peeking out from behind some fluffy white clouds, and we saw a blue sky. Having our heavier clothes on, we were dressed too warm and soon had to remove a layer.

This hike turned out to be one of the easier ones. Crossing at DeWitt Road, we entered into a rather bushy area that soon turned into a nice wooded area for quite a distance. The trail was well marked and well taken care of, and we hiked right along. We were happy to see so many squirrels. Today we counted twenty.

We walked along and crossed over a railway track and along above the track and up a hill. Far above us was a huge cross on the top of the hill. We didn't know if it was permanent or had been put there for the Christmas season, which was fast approaching. Upon further investigation, we discovered the ten-meter (33 ft) high metal cross was erected in 1966, in commemoration of a priest. The cross has 106 light bulbs along the edges and is lit up every night of the year. Although originally it was only to be lit for six weeks during Christmas and Easter.

Close by is the Devil's Punch Bowl, believed to be named so because of the moonshiners setting up shop on the road to the punch bowl, and when they got thirsty, they would go to the falls for cold water. We did not take the side trail to see the Devil's Punch Bowl, as the side trips usually consisted of at least two hours, and we never felt we could afford the time. We next came to Battlefield Park, named in commemoration of the site of a British victory in the War of 1812. What an area of history! This park had camping facilities as well as picnic tables, barbeque facilities, washrooms, and drinking water. We appreciated the washrooms!

Before starting up the long incline to the top of the escarpment, we stopped for lunch and a rest. After our usual fare, we climbed up the incline and came upon a beautiful sight called Felkers Falls. We stopped to take some pictures and to enjoy the view.

Hiking over rocks, roots, crevices, etc., one cannot take one's eyes off the trail in front of you for fear of stumbling and ending up on the ground. This necessitates stopping to view your surroundings and enjoying the great outdoors, which adds to the time it takes to finish the hike. The falls were fed by a lively stream, and we didn't see too many of those, as it had been quite a dry summer. The falls dropped by steps to midway and then cascaded down to the streambed about seventy-five to a hundred feet below.

We followed the stream and crossed over a steel bridge and entered a trail for the physically handicapped called Peter Street Trail, which provided a beautiful view of Felkers Falls, the city of Hamilton, Ontario, and Lake Ontario below.

Emerging from the conservation area, we entered an open area and skirted a park and a subdivision and crossed Mount Albion Road and slowly descended back down the escarpment. We met an elderly man and his daughter and their dog. Always eager to engage in some interaction with the canine side of life, we conversed with the dog as well as the gentleman who informed us he had completed the Bruce Trail twice. He also told us of a couple he had met during one of his hikes who had hiked the trail seven times. I believe once, for us, will be sufficient.

We continued through another lovely area of large trees and ended up in an open area, which was once a ski run. Following along to the bottom edge, we eventually climbed back up and finished our day at 2:30 p.m. at the meeting place on Mountain Brow Boulevard and the Mohawk Access Trail parking area. Mary arrived soon after at 2:45 p.m. (we were happy to see her) and drove back to pick up our cars at MacDui Drive. We had spied a Tim Horton's on our way, so we headed back for a bit of a snack before leaving for home.

It had been a really good hike, crossing four or five streams (with actual water in them), a flock of mourning doves, the squirrels, a few people and dogs, and, of course, more beautiful views.

We may try for one more before Old Man Winter sets in. If not, spring 2003 will see us back again (all three hopefully) hiking the Bruce and having a wonderful time doing it.

We have now traveled 122.4 km. We only have 700 km plus left to go.

Hike No. 12

April 19, 2003

It was April 19, 2003. It was also my eldest daughter's birthday. It was a Saturday and the first walk of 2003. We began at Iroquois Heights Conservation Area where we had walked on November 24, 2002. We certainly felt we were much more seasoned hikers now than we were then. Bernice and I met, still missing Mary, on a lovely spring morning at 9:00 a.m. with some light cloud cover, but it was a really nice day for hiking.

We started out along the brow of the mountain and soon came to a sharp right turn, through some woods, and then through an open area, which was very muddy and wet. We came to Highway 403, which now has a nice bridge over it. We continued up the slight rise through the woods with lots of wildlife compared with some of our other hikes. There were lots of chipmunks, squirrels, and birds, mainly cardinals and chickadees.

We crossed a creek, ascended the ridge, and then quickly descended to Wilson Street. This section was a little difficult, especially near the top, when I offered my assistance to give Bernice a boost over some rocks, which sent her on her nose. Despite my apology, she did not ask for my help the rest of the hike. We crossed Wilson Street and checked the time and our approximate distance. We were surprised to see we had gone 4 km in just about two hours. Of course, we had been stopping and chatting every few yards on our walk and talk, as Bernice called it. We decided to put forth more effort into the walk and a little less into the talk. We walked along the edge of Wilson Street for a few yards and started downhill, only to find the trail started back up and, after about twenty minutes, were back at the top of Wilson Street. Funny how that happens!

From there we crossed over Tiffany Creek and the lovely Sherman Falls, on through another wooded area to Old Dundas Road

Bernice at Sherman Falls Hike #12 2003

Just ahead were a group of motorcyclists taking a break and also some pictures of themselves. We decided to do the same. Crossing a wooden and steel bridge at these falls, we climbed a good height to the top ridge again. We began to think of something to eat, and as we came to some huge rock formations, we stopped for our lunch. It was 12:15 p.m., and we enjoyed the view and our lunch until 1:00 p.m. We saw lots of people being lured out to enjoy the sights and sounds of spring. We particularly noticed the very bright green foliage on the evergreen trees, no longer the dark green shades we had become accustomed to during the winter. We were also surprised at the amount of water gurgling and splashing along the creek and streambeds.

As we began again, we came to the Violet Williams Plaque and turned sharp right along a lovely wide pathway leading to the Hermitage Ruins.

Heritage Ruins Hike #12 2003

This was once a summer home of a family from Hamilton, Ontario. It was a beautiful setting atop a gentle rise, surrounded by lofty trees, beautiful evergreens, and lovely green lawns. One could imagine horses and carriages arriving on a lovely summer day, bringing guests from the heat of the city to the cool shaded countryside in the mid-1800s.

Following on the trail and through the woods, we soon came to a decline crossing over Sulphur Creek, and there waiting for us was Bernice's friend Jim Burr. Jim became our go to guy whenever we needed to be picked up.

Jim Our Always Willing Driver Hike #12 2003

We were surprised how well we felt and how quickly we had completed our twelfth hike, a total of 10.7 km in just four and a half hours. Jim drove us to our cars, and we changed into more presentable clothes and met up at McDonald's at a large mall at the junction of Mohawk Road and Alexander Parkway. After a nice visit with Jim and a light lunch, we bade good-bye with some possible dates set for our next hike.

I arrived home at 4:30 p.m., surprising my husband, who had calculated a 6:00 p.m. return. It just proves we are becoming seasoned hikers—finally. We have now a total of 133.1 km completed.

Hike No. 13

May 5, 2003

It was Monday, May 5, 2003. It should have been Friday, the thirteenth. Why did we not think that hike no. 13 might end up being bad luck? We were naïve, and it never occurred to us to even be a little extra cautious.

So on a happy note, we started out, albeit late, due to my again missing my turns, etc. I ended up going the wrong way on Mohawk Road off Lincoln Alexander Parkway. Then I turned off on to Mineral Springs Road. I should have veered off to the right on Sulphur Springs Road." Too many Springs Roads. After many, many traffic lights and much traffic on Mohawk and a couple of phone calls to Bernice to alert her that I was indeed on my way, I finally met with Bernice at the Dundas Conservation parking lot. Looking back, it is absolutely amazing we actually finished this trail.

The day was dull, and it was predicted that there was an 80 percent chance of rain, but we thought we would be done and safely ensconced in our cars before the rain could catch up with us. We will discuss the rain later. The temperature was around 10°C, which was a very good hiking temperature for us.

Once we got under way, we headed up a steep hill and across the rail line into a wooded area. An old railway station (on the old Toronto, Hamilton, Buffalo line) is now a center for history, flora and fauna, and surrounding nature trails. We crossed ski loops and came out on Governor's Road. Because it is a very busy thoroughfare, we walked down the road apiece before we crossed over. Up an old road, there was a horse farm to our right and some lovely horses grazing on the rolling hills, which was a nice sight.

Descending down into a rather marshy area, we encountered marsh marigolds, and as we started climbing again, there was a large patch of trilliums. We also saw lots of squirrels and birds this time and even a Jack-in-the-Pulpit, which is very rare these days unless you go deep into the countryside. We came out of the woods at King Street in Dundas at a very steep hill, so we walked down a few yards and over the other side and up to the main CN line and higher, leaving the valley behind. We had a lovely view of Dundas as we went along to Spencer Creek, which leads to the base of Webster's Falls.

Webster Falls Hike #13 2003.

We then climbed approximately thirty steps hewn out of the rock to a one hundred and twenty three step metal staircase and another thirty steps to reach the top. Who needs "Stair Master"?

The falls were lovely and the parkland around very clean and well kept, with a lovely cobblestone bridge over Spencer Creek. We stayed there for our lunch, sitting on a bench that encircled a large tree. We had just about finished when a little pitter-patter of rain began to fall. At

12:45 p.m., after about a thirty-minute break (which we needed after the steps), we crossed the bridge and came to an iron-fenced cemetery where the Webster family is buried. The whole area was once the property of the Webster family in the 1800s and is a beautiful tribute to their name. Tews Falls was the next highlight, which is nearly as high as Niagara Falls but with a much smaller water flow. From this point I believe is when we went on to the Dundas Peak Side Trail and ended up where we definitely did not want to be. Not really knowing where we were (what else is new?), we walked down into the town of Dundas, and it was raining quite hard by this time. As we were hiking along, water dripping off our sleeves and our faces and looking thoroughly soaked, a young woman came along in her station wagon. We stopped her and asked her how to get to Rock Chapel Road. She must have thought we were crazy, because it was a few miles back to where we were supposed to be. She very nicely offered to drive us to our destination, which at first we declined due to our awful appearance, but she insisted (taking pity on a couple of old ladies), so we relented ever so happily. Mother Nature must have taken pity on us as well, seeing the mess we were in, and sent us a Good Samaritan.

As a footnote, the Bruce Trail guide issues new maps, now and again, as trails are altered for various reasons. Sometimes people allow access to their private property, or areas become dangerous due to soil erosion, etc. There had been changes to the trail in this area, and this was what happened to us, as we were hiking from an old guide and missed the new trails.

We arrived at the Rock Chapel Road parking lot and Mary had not yet arrived. Our Good Samaritan didn't want to leave us, but we insisted Mary would soon be along, and indeed she was. We thanked our kind driver, and wondered as she drove off what would have happened if she hadn't come to our aid. We were so happy to see Mary. Seeing how wet and cold we were, she turned on the heater, which helped to warm and dry us out a little bit. Fortunately, we had a change of clothes in our cars but decided to skip our usual early dinner get-together and just head on home. We each arrived at our destinations around 5:00 p.m. We always checked to make sure we all arrived home safe and sound. In spite of the rain, getting lost, etc., we had finished our hike in good time, approximately five hours.

This was another very memorable hike. I was sorry not to have a chance to visit with Mary, but we planned our fourteenth hike for May

19. (This would take place only if there was not an 80 percent chance of rain). We were again alerted to the fact that you must keep an eagle eye on the blazes and know *exactly* which way you are going. Bernice quickly requested updated maps for future reference.

We had completed 12.9 km of hiking and several more hopping a ride. Balance is now approximately 660 km. It's still a long way to Tobermory (song title: "It's a Long Way to Tipperary"). Only folks our age will remember that one! So until next time . . .

Hike No. 14

May 19, 2003

Oh, what a beautiful morning,
Oh, what a beautiful day . . .
I've got a beautiful feeling,
Everything's going my way!

Yes, yes, it certainly was a beautiful morning, a Monday morning, May 19, 2003. We started out from the parking lot on Rock Chapel Road and headed west, crossing the road over Borer's Creek, with a fantastic view of Borer's Falls. Not a wide falls but very high. As we looked over the edge of the falls, we viewed a raccoon but high up in the crux of a tree having a lovely morning nap in the warm sunshine. What a sight! No doubt he was tired out from a night of moonlighting.

From here we entered into the Royal Botanical Gardens property in Burlington, Ontario, consisting of almost 3,000 acres of parks, walkways, and gardens. The gardens were created in the 1930s and have increasingly added and created new features over the years. They now contain beautiful lilacs, fragrant in the spring, rose gardens in full bloom from late June to mid-September. Numerous other flowers beds, such as irises, peonies, lilies, rhododendrons, and azaleas all flaunt their beauty throughout the seasons. There are many activities throughout the year, a food and wine festival, the Ontario Garden Show in April, and the Rose Society Show in June. There is also the Gardens Café, a teahouse, and a pavilion; and the gardens offer visitors many hours of horticultural splendor.

As we hiked along the brow of the escarpment, we veered to a more northerly direction and came upon a great view of the city of Hamilton and the Burlington Skyway. We descended down a steep decline with a railing into a wooded area, crossed over a stream, and steadily climbed back up again. We encountered a little girl and her father hiking, and the height of the steps was almost a high as she was. We took a picture of them and said if it turned out we would send them a copy.

Crossing over Valley Road and enjoying the wooded areas and the swampy sumac areas, we came to Patterson Road. As we started upward again, there were trilliums in profusion. There were more up and down rocky areas, and then we arrived at Snake Road. Just the name of it gave me the willies! I can't believe we stopped here for our lunch. Fortunately, we didn't encounter any snakes. We watched numerous mountain bikers ride by, covered with mud but happy. We were still in the botanical gardens. Being a very rocky, hilly stretch, we were very glad we were walking and not biking. As we lunched, some folks came by with a young dog, which ran right up to me and jumped on me as if I was an old friend. Being just a pup, she was very rambunctious. Fortunately, I love dogs because she had come from behind me and startled me. We had a friendly little interaction, and the dog was off to find another friend. We had taken about thirty minutes for our lunch, so we packed up at 12:45 p.m. and started out again. It was getting very warm.

After we crossed Snake Road, we circled a very large swampy area and eventually came to a bridge crossing Grindstone Creek. What a creek! It was a very fast-flowing waterway, tumbling over huge rocks which again reminded us of the force of the glaciers moving such huge pieces of rocks. There were some steep climbs here and a good number of people out for a Monday-afternoon communing with nature. After a very steep climb, we arrived at the beautiful picturesque Waterdown Falls. And as usual, Mary was waiting for us.

We changed our clothes and headed to Clappisons Corners (after first picking up our cars at Chapel Rock Road) and enjoyed a break at Wendy's before we headed for home. We agreed we would try to add some more kilometers in a couple of weeks. We had hiked 10.4 km.

HIKE NO. 15

June 15, 2003

The hike was planned for June 6, 2003, but after encountering a couple of setbacks it was delayed until June 15th. It was a Sunday and Father's Day. My husband, being the good sport that he is, didn't mind my spending Father's Day hiking through the countryside, and besides, I was bringing Mary back with me for dinner and to spend the night, as she had an appointment the next day in St. Catharines, Ontario, and we would all be able to have a nice visit.

Previously, Bernice had developed a heavy cold, and I had experienced an attack of vertigo. Being dizzy is one thing you don't want to be when hiking over those hills and rocks. Besides, I wouldn't have wanted Bernice to turn around and find me missing, having tumbled off into nowhere! So having recuperated, we met at Waterdown Falls at 9:00 a.m. and went off in good time with long sleeves, long pants, and plenty of bug spray, as we were in the midst of mosquito season.

It was a lovely day—sunny, low humidity, 24°C. However, due to the previous days of excessive rain, we were soon slugging through mud like we had never encountered before. We crossed over Mill Street and entered up a hill into a lovely housing subdivision. Skirting the field behind the houses, we turned west and slugged through more mud for several meters. We followed an old practice trotting track and went back into the woods. We had a minor first-aid stop along this route. Bernice had scratched her hand after being struck by a thorny bush. We performed the "salve and a Band-Aid" thing and continued on. (My children well remember the “salve and a Band-Aid” thing, as it averted many a crisis.)

Arriving at Kerns Road, we stopped for a midmorning break at around 10:30 a.m.—time to rest the legs after all that mud slugging. We then descended a short, steep hill into a hardwood valley. This part was quite nice, with several short ups and downs. Not difficult though. It was about 2 km long. We stopped for lunch in this area and were surrounded by forget-me-nots. What a lovely sight!

We crossed Halton Road 5 (a very busy four-lane highway) and entered back into the woods, eventually reaching Guelph Line. Mary was waiting, and it was a good thing that we were pretty much on time at 2:30 p.m. because the parking area was just a car width at the side of the road. We drove along, looking for a parking spot for our cars for the beginning of our next walk. We were planning on a July 6 date. We had completed 11 km this day.

We returned to our cars at Waterdown Falls and stopped at an old inn in Waterdown for a bit of a mid-afternoon lunch. After a good visit, we left for home. Mary followed me back to Niagara Falls to celebrate Father’s Day.

Another successful day in the odyssey of the Bruce Trail hikers!

Hike No. 16

May 6, 2004

Well, we finally made it—the return to hiking the Bruce and the beginning of 2004. We had to postpone our hiking for the balance of 2003, as I had badly twisted my ankle, and hiking was out of the question. I spent almost six months in therapy but returned to the trail as good as new.

It was Thursday, May 6, 2004, and a perfect day for hiking. We met at Mount Nemo Conservation Park. There was a large parking lot with room for a hundred cars and large maps of the area. We were to meet at 9:00 a.m., but both arrived around 8:40 a.m. (eager or what?). However, by the time we got in our boots and got the rest of our gear together, it was near 9:00 a.m. We were reversing our trail this time and headed north for a while and then south to our destination.

It seemed like we had hardly begun when we reached Harris Point, a wonderful panorama of the Hamilton, Toronto skyline. Continuing on along the edge of the escarpment, we crisscrossed over several fissures, some leading to deep vertical caves. Here, the trail came to a steep rock decline, I took one look and said, "Well, there must be some other way."

Rocky Descent Hike #16 2004.

We had to climb down about fifteen feet between two huge rock formations. It was a sight! Realizing there was no other way, Bernice bravely climbed down first, successfully. I passed down all our gear and then began my decline. Bernice wanted to photograph the event. With my body wedged sideways and my foot dangling about four feet off the ground, it was a photo Bernice really wanted to shoot. We were laughing so hard, and Bernice was having trouble getting the view in the view finder, and I was trying to find some footing. Our laughter really slowed the progress. We finally got on with it and soon came to a narrow dirt road and were astounded to find we were arriving at our destination, and it was only 10:30 a.m. Some miscalculations somewhere!

Mary was going to pick us up at 1:00 p.m., so we had a long wait. We chatted and took a short hike up Walker's Line, returned to a nice shaded area off Walker's Line, and ate our lunches. Surprisingly, Mary soon arrived. She wanted to arrive early and read a book in the quiet of the countryside. We foiled that plan. It was fun all the same. Mary drove us to our cars although we stopped en route at Tim Horton's (I said they were all over the place) and had lunch and visited some more before heading for home. We had a short but successful hike, completing approximately a total 172.5 km at this point, and we planned to hike again either on May 12 or 14. Till then . . .

Hike No. 17

May 16, 2004

Sunday, May 16, was a lovely spring morning—just a little nip in the air but perfect for a good day of hiking. We started at the Mount Nemo Conservation parking lot after two delays. The previous Wednesday and Friday had not worked out for us. We headed down Colling Road, right to Blind Line and approximately 2 km on to Britannia Road, passing by some gorgeous rural properties. Of course, with all the spring flowers and trees in full bloom, Mother Nature was at her very best. Wonderful-smelling lilac bushes enhanced the whole experience.

We crossed over the fast-flowing Bronte Creek on a high steel bridge. Shortly, we came to a one-hundred-meter boardwalk through a swamp. It was dried up in spite of what we had thought was a pretty wet spring. Climbing up from the valley was rather steep, but we took our time, stopping to admire the many trilliums growing through the wooded area. Exiting this wooded area brought us to the village of Kilbride. Passing a school and some sports fields, we again entered the bush and crossed another brisk lively stream and arrived at Derry Road. Crossing over Derry Road, we climbed to the edge of a farming area. Also some calcium pits were interesting to see, and so were some very clean-looking and good-sized ponds. We stopped for our lunch at this part of the trail and, soon after, arrived at Twiss Road.

At the parking area on Twiss Road, we found Jim waiting for us, and he had brought a wonderful surprise of Krispy Kreme donuts. This was a new fad that had taken over some areas of Southern Ontario. Bernice had tasted them, but I hadn't (they hadn't reached Niagara yet). After devouring two of the best donuts ever, Jim drove us to our cars, stopping en route for coffee in a lovely little bistro. Having already eaten our lunches and the KK donuts, coffee was all we could manage. Jim had not had lunch though, so he opted for some highly recommended pancakes and syrup. We were all surprised when a plate of three eight-inch-wide and three-quarter-inch thick pancakes arrived. Jim tackled them, but they were simply more than he could handle.

Next to the bistro was an artisan's workshop. The artist had put his talents to work in the bistro. As you entered, there was a lovely waterfall against the wall, falling into a shallow pool. In the ladies' washroom was a lovely corner hand basin made from some kind of rock brought in from the Peterborough, Ontario, area. The shop was closed, but it would be interesting to see more of his creations at some future time.

As it was time to head home, we said our good-byes with plans to hike again very soon. That day, we had hiked 11.3 km.

Hike No. 18

May 28, 2004

We followed up last week's hike with this one on Friday, May 28, 2004. We started on Twiss Road at the Calcium Pits on a lovely morning. We wore short sleeves and light nylon jackets sprayed with insect repellant. Right off the hop, we started climbing upward from the road over steep rocks for about five minutes. I dropped my water bottle down between some large fissures in the rock. Bernice was able to retrieve it for me. I did not look forward to a long hike without any water. Somehow I perceived that maybe we were in for a rather rough day.

The trail was a challenge. Sometimes extremely rocky areas made for slow progress. Other times the trails were wide and easy. The whole area was extremely well marked. We agreed it was probably the best marked trail to date. We came to an area that overlooks the Nassagawega Canyon. This deep valley was formed during the Ice Age, approximately 12,000-13,500 years ago. This melting carved the canyon, which is 144 feet deep. This area is called the Milton Outlier. It was once a part of the escarpment, but corrosive action from an ancient stream separated it from the escarpment. Looking across to the opposite side, one sees nothing but trees.

We left that beautiful view and descended to Walker's Line road allowance, across Limestone Creek, a remnant of the glacial torrents. The trail climbs gradually up the Nassagawega Canyon wall to Rattlesnake Point Side Trail. This side trail is one of about five other side trails just on this stretch of our hike.

It was close to noon, so we sat on the side of the trail to have our lunch and were surprised by some eighty high school students bursting forth from the bush on a field outing. We laughed when they passed by because Bernice (for some unknown reason) had her unsheathed hunting knife lying beside her. I guess we scared them!

The day became overcast, but it was good hiking weather. Somehow I developed a blister on my heel, so we stopped a couple of times for Band-Aid application. We had so far been very lucky not to suffer anything but very minor physical problems. We continued north along the canyon rim and entered a beautiful pine and oak woods and then abruptly turned into a wooded and swampy area. We continued along the edge of Milton Heights with lovely views of the valley below and eventually came to a high rocky flat surface just above Glen Eden Ski Slopes in the Kelso Conservation Area. From here we could see Kelso Lake and the parking lot and hoped Mary would be waiting for us. It was around 2:15 p.m., and after five hours of hiking, we were ready for a leisurely rest. We hiked down the ski slope and entered the parking lot and began to look for Mary's car. There were lots of cars, but alas, none was hers. Bernice chatted with a couple of girls who worked for the park, and the only entrance was about 0.5 km back from where we had come down the slope. Heading back, we realized I didn't have my cell phone and we couldn't contact Mary. What a predicament! While we sat and contemplated what we should do, a young man approached us and asked if we were looking for a lady in a tan car. Voila—Mary! Mother Nature again opted to help out a couple of well-worn-out hikers. Mary had been waiting for us at the top of an escarpment in another park's parking lot. This friendly fellow kindly offered to drive us to that parking lot. As we were placing our gear in the trunk, lo and behold, there was a beautiful Mountie hat resting in the trunk.

We asked if he was indeed a member of the Royal Canadian Mounted Police, and he was. So it turned out that old adage was true—a Mountie always gets his man (well, woman)! Two even! He drove us up the hill, and we met Mary at the park entrance. We thanked our Mountie for helping two very grateful hikers and climbed into Mary's car for the ride back to our cars. Could we possibly be any luckier?

Bernice was eager to get home, as her nephew was working on her deck, but we arranged for a tentative date of June 6 to continue. Mary and I ended up at the little bistro in Lowville and enjoyed sandwiches in this delightful little restaurant. I arrived home at six thirty tired and happy to be home. It had been a good day and a 12.6 km hike. We were nearing the 200 km point of our hike and were happy to have achieved this much and anxiously looking forward to the rest. Hope we make it. With the help of farmers, hikers, Mounties, and others (on future hikes), we always managed to finish our hike. Providence must be helping out too, because we sure confound ourselves.

Hike No. 19

June 6, 2004

This was another hike to remember, although nearly all of them were. I had spent three days visiting my friend Jane in Bobcageon, Ontario, so I approached the starting point from an entirely different direction. I arose on Sunday, June 6, at 5:10 a.m. at Jane's and headed out by 5:40 a.m. on a rather cool overcast morning. After a two-and-half-hour drive, I arrived at our meeting place at the Kelso Conservation Area three quarters of an hour early. Unknown to us it was a triathlon race day at Kelso, and we weren't allowed in the park. This turned out to be okay for us, because we parked at the entrance and didn't have to pay a parking fee.

As the cyclists and runners threaded their way along their path, we started out on ours at precisely 9:00 a.m. We encountered some young runners but were soon on our own. We entered the woods after leaving a stretch of Appleby Line and crossed under Highway 401 onto Campbellville Road. This ends the Iroquois section and begins the Toronto section of the trail.

After crossing Campbellville Road, we began our climb up the escarpment under the power lines stretching north from the mighty Niagara. From this point, we could see Kelso Lake and the Toronto skyline. We climbed over a stile and skirted the Halton County Golf Club and ended up on 6th Line. We laughed because we could have just walked over to the golf course and followed 6th Line to our destination instead of plodding over hill and dale.

We began our trek over stone fissures and tree roots for many a careful step, as we were edging along the escarpment, and one wouldn't want to lose one's footing there. Although we had to be cautious, we couldn't help but marvel at the rocks and the trees clinging to them. Amazingly, these trees are upward of five hundred years old and, of course, the rocks many million years older. Makes one feel very insignificant!

We came to a forty-foot bridge span at the Dufferin Quarry.

Forty Foot Bridge Span Quarry Hike #19 2004

The bridge was funded and built by corporations and private and public sponsors in the early 1990s. There is a plaque and a display describing quarrying and the geology of the Niagara escarpment. This quarry is huge and is dug out by huge machines to crush rocks to various sizes of gravel and sand. The bridge was about one hundred feet high, and we laughingly remarked we were glad it wasn't a swing bridge. We stopped for a quick lunch and a repair job of Bernice's toe, which wanted to become blistered. I thought she was just being a copycat, since I had had a blister during last hike. It seemed to be more difficult with the continual walking over these rock fissures and roots from the trees.

We had to be very wary of our steps. Progress was slow, and we were running out of time. Jim was scheduled to meet us at approximately 1:30-2:00 p.m. It was almost 2:00 p.m., and we still had 2 km to go.

We arrived at St. Helena Road, which took us out to Regional Road 25. We called Jim to advise him of our location, and as we turned to head for the road, Jim drove by us. He had only been a few hundred yards around the bend in the road. We drove to our cars after a quick coffee and soon said our farewells. We totaled 12.7 km this day. We were getting there, step by step.

Hike No. 20

June 13, 2004

What a perfect beginning. Bernice and I arrived at 15th Sideroad at 8:28 a.m. on Sunday, June 13, 2004, at exactly the same time. Talk about timing! A 28°C day was predicted, so we wanted to get an early start. It was overcast and just fine for short sleeves and mosquito jackets, as we were in the midst of mosquito weather. After donning our hiking boots and checking our gear, we started off at about 8:45 a.m. right into the bush a few yards past Speyside on 15th Sideroad.

The route started up a small incline but quickly leveled off and became a very pleasant walk. We passed a couple of side trails and came to 3rd Line, crossed over 17th Sideroad, and continued on 3rd Line through some swampy and muddy areas. We were making excellent time and thoroughly enjoying our hike.

We stopped for a wee break and some energy food at a stile and then skirted two sides of a farmer's field, coming to another stile into a second field. This field was being worked by a young lad on a tractor, and as we came to a third field, the farmer was leaning against his tractor. We stopped to chat, and he told us that because the field was so wet he was unable to bundle the hay like he was hoping to. He was hoping for some sun and wind to dry up the hay before some more rain came. As we chatted, two young women came along with their dog, also hiking the Bruce. We found out that, like us, they had started the trail at Queenston, Ontario. They were at the same point as us, but they had just started the hike this past April. Are we slow or what? You can see what a few years in age can make! We probably could have done 20 km a day for two days every weekend too when we were forty to fifty years younger. It's been three years ago this August since we started. We are still going, and that is something to be proud of, don't you agree?

We continued chatting with Farmer Brown (could be his name) and finding out about his cattle prices on the stock market, etc. He told us he bought his herd for $1.18 a pound and they were now being sold at 84¢ per pound. Not good money. It was all because of finding one mad cow being diseased. After about half an hour, we decided to carry on and thanked our farmer friend for allowing us hikers to tread over his fields. We left the farm via another stile, crossed 5th Line and found a shady, grassy spot to stop for lunch.

Feeling refreshed and eager to continue, we climbed up some rocks and entered the Limehouse Conservation Area. We hiked over some fissures and came upon an area called Hole in the Wall. There are two ladders in an area about 10-12 feet down between two huge rock formations.

Opening thru Fissures Hike 20 2004

At the bottom of the hill is a trail called the Guelph Radial Trail. It is so called because it heads west from Limehouse along the route of the Old Toronto Suburban Radial Railway. We crossed over Black Creek and saw the remains of an old mill and, farther along, a huge old lime kiln, one of three in the area. These lime kilns supplied lime for every possible construction job in early Upper Canada. The introduction of railroads and the loss of the trees needed for stoking the kilns saw the end of the kilns by early 1900.

We came out of this section at the village of Limestone on Halton Regional Road 43 and 5th Line. At the intersection was a small park, and we sat down on benches amid lovely flower beds and waited for Mary. It was 1:00 p.m. Mary arrived at 1:15 p.m., and we made our way to a Tim Horton's and had a little lunch in Acton, Ontario. We soon headed back to our cars and home for another day.

We checked to make sure we each had our proper belongings and said our good-byes with a plan to hike again very soon. I thought it was interesting also that as we reached the intersection of Road 25 and 15th Sideroad, Bernice turned left (west) to 401 and home, Mary turned right (east) on the way to Acton and Highway 7 for Kitchener, Ontario (via Guelph, Ontario), and I went straight through on 15th Sideroad to Guelph Line and left to Queen Elizabeth Way and home. It had been an interesting hike, we had some interesting conversations, and we had completed 8.9 km, totaling 205.5 km to date. We will try for June 25 for our twenty-first hike.

Hike No. 21

June 25, 2004

On Friday, June 25, 2004, we started out around 8:45 a.m. on a beautiful morning. The traffic was pretty heavy until we came to a hilly area, and then it lessened to almost no traffic at all. Probably people had already gone to work and the children were gone to school. Bernice and I both arrived at our destination within minutes of each other; however, Bernice arrived first as usual.

After getting our gear together—boots, walking sticks, backpacks, etc.—we headed over the bridge, which took us over the railway and left up to 5th Line for about 1.5km then over a stile into the bush. Long stretches of boardwalks assisted our walk over the swampy areas. There were no rocks, roots, etc., for a change. We hiked along to 6th Line and on to Highway 7 and then along the highway for a few minutes. We passed a nice little motel on the highway and then soon turned back into the woods. Again, we encountered more swampy areas, with lots of boardwalks, making the hike really easy. We did not take time to visit the Scotsdale Farm, a shorthorn beef farm operated by the Ontario Heritage Foundation from a donation by the Bennett family.

Nearing 8th Line, we came across some Jack-in-the-Pulpits, which we had not seen this year but had seen some last June, a lovely little plant that grows in wooded areas. Here, we stopped and had our lunch even though it was only 11:45 a.m. We were surprised we had made such good time.

We were looking at a huge map that was located here, and after some consideration, we decided we would shorten our hike and avoid more flat, mossy rocks. (We were certainly more than familiar with them). We crossed 8th Line to 27th Sideroad and headed north on this lovely country road. With such good footing, we could really take in the scenery. We stopped at Snow Creek, a pretty little creek tumbling over a couple of waterfalls on one side of the road and then dropping down the escarpment on the other side. Had we continued along the actual trail, we would have descended down the escarpment, crossed the creek, and ascended back up again. We just circumvented this way and soon came to 9th Line and the Silver Creek Education Centre.

It was only 12:45 p.m., and Jim was coming at around 2:00 p.m. We enjoyed sitting on one of the picnic benches and actually felt a bit cold (even on this late date in June) due to clouds that passed over. About 2:00 p.m., Bernice called Jim on his cell phone. They were having some difficulty communicating, but we were hoping he would soon locate us. He was having a difficult time finding us because no one seemed to know of this Silver Creek Centre. It is actually owned by the Dufferin-Peel Catholic District School Board and is used for outings and retreats.

Jim finally located us and thoughtfully brought us each a chocolate bar to get us energized for the trip back to our cars. Despite our shortcut and our wait for Jim, we had a great day. We will start at this Silver Creek Centre hopefully on July 18, for our twenty-second hike. We are now at the 218.7 km mark on the trail, completing 13.2 km on this trip.

Hike No. 22

July 18, 2004

We had planned to do this section on July 18, 2004, and indeed our plan worked for us, and this Sunday morning we were to start our way from the Silver Creek Education Centre where we last finished. This center was in the middle of nowhere, down winding back roads of the Credit Valley area. Actually, you follow Fallbrook Trail north of 27 Sideroad. I did, however, manage to find my way there and arrived at around 8:30 a.m., fully expecting Bernice to be waiting for me. She hadn't arrived yet, so as I exited the car surveyed my surroundings, I was puzzled by a tapping noise breaking the solitude of the early morning. When I began to investigate, I was startled to see eight vultures perched on a tin roof of a shed behind me and approximately six or eight more circling the area. Obviously, they were looking for breakfast! It was an eerie feeling in the silence of this out-of-the-way place, and I jumped back in the car, not wanting to be the breakfast they were looking for. When Bernice arrived, she agreed that it felt very strange to be amid ugly-looking large birds eyeing us in this quiet, isolated area.

Not wanting to linger any longer than necessary with the ugly ones, we set out at about 9:00 a.m. and began our hike, turning off 9th Line into the woods two to three hundred meters down the road from the center, taking us to the top of the escarpment. We saw some very small red mushroom-type fungus, which we certainly wouldn't add to our lunch menu. We stopped for a break at 10th Line around 10:15 a.m. As we hiked along 10th Line, we came past a huge house with large ponds and what looked like tents. We were in the Terra Cotta Conservation Area, and hiking back and forth along the valley and crossing several bridges, we came to the Terra Cotta Interpretive Centre. We crossed a parking lot to Winston Churchill Boulevard. It was close to 1:00 p.m. Crossing the road, we again headed up to the brow of the escarpment into a large maple woodlot. Continuing along this trail, we had a fairly comfortable hike and came out at Boston Mills Road. We followed this north to Mississauga Road, where Jim picked us up. We drove back to our cars and, without further ado, headed for home. Except for the vultures, it had been a rather ho-hum hike. We had hiked 12.7 km and completed 231.4 km. We hoped to do another section sometime in August.

Hike No. 23

August 21,2004

Well, we finally got hiking again on Saturday, August 21, 2004, in the Caledon Hills area. I arrived at the town of Inglewood at around 9:00 a.m. and missed the parking area, and as I waited on the main street, Bernice did the exact same thing as I had done, so I realized she would be back in a couple of minutes. I flagged her down, and we decided to park in the local arena parking lot. There did not seem to be any place to start, so we asked a local where the trail started. It was up the road a few yards. We donned our gear and headed down the rail trail. It is actually the old Canadian National Beeton Railway Line.

It was certainly a treat to just follow a flat, straight-ahead trail, crossing side roads as we came to them at about 1.5 km intervals. We crossed Kennedy Road, Heart Lake Road, Horseshoe Hill Road, and St. Andrews Road and stopped each time for a mini-break. Surprisingly, it is in some ways more difficult to walk on a long straight trail as it is to climb up and down for some distance. We tend to walk a little faster on the flat, which seems to put a little extra pressure on the old body after a while.

We continued on, uneventfully, until we saw Jim waiting in the distance. When we got to him, we asked if he had been waiting long. He said he had been waiting a while but had asked a cyclist if she had seen a couple of women hiking along, and she said she had seen a couple of "old ladies." We thank you very much! We are, at least, still able to walk the trail and don't have to sit down and pedal our way along the Bruce!

Jim drove around and found a little restaurant on Hurontario Road (Highway 10), and we stopped for a bite to eat. This little place was a going concern and only stayed open until 3:00 p.m. on Saturdays, so we just had time to order and eat before they closed. Good food too!

It had been a beautiful hiking day, but we were anxious to head home. Back to our cars, Bernice headed to Highway 24, and I took the 403 to the Queen Elizabeth Way and on home. It now takes about two hours' travel time each way.

We finished at Centreville Creek Road around 1:45 p.m., completing 13.2 km for the day. Our total now stands at 244.6 km. We will try for Sunday, September 15, for our next hike.

Hike No. 24

September 15, 2004

It was hike no. 24, Wednesday, September 15, 2004, 22°C, and we were in the Albion Hills Conservation Area. The weather was ideal but was completely overcast. However, there was a lovely breeze. We expected rain but did not take our rainwear with us. Amazingly, we both arrived at the starting point at exactly the same time and started out just around 9:20 a.m. We have been fortunate or determined or maybe just lucky to keep our starting times at around 9:00-9:30 a.m.

We made good time on the last 4 km part of the rail trail, completing it in less than an hour. Turning left onto Duffy's Lane, we followed it and then turned into the Palgrave Conservation Area. This was a reforestation area presenting a lovely wide pine-needle floor and a peaceful quietness. The tall pines were trimmed of their lower branches and rose to seventy or eighty feet. A breeze and a soft rustle of leaves escorted us along the way.

We arrived at Gore Road and again followed the road for four hundred meters before climbing a stile into a meadow. There were more large pine trees, and then a swampy area was made easy by walking on the boardwalk. We arrived at Centreville Creek Road. Next, we came to cedars and some more swampy areas and more boardwalks. We had encountered two or three cyclists on the trail, but once we started into the wooded area, we didn't see anyone else all day, which wasn't all that unusual.

Around 1:00 p.m., the sun finally burst through the overcast sky, bringing increased warmth with it. We covered two meadows and began to feel the heat of the sun. The trail climbed the escarpment, and we had a lovely view of the Oak Ridges Moraine, where I took a picture of Bernice to finish off our film. We could have taken *my* picture and entitled it "Lorraine on the Moraine."

Bernice on the Moraine Hike #24 2004

Anyway, we hiked a kilometer or so more through yet another hardwood bush and ended up on Coolihands Road, where Mary was waiting this time.

Mary drove us to our cars, and we continued on to an eatery in East Caledon and had a cool drink and a visit. Bernice headed out first to pick up a purchase she had made in Erin, Ontario. (She actually got lost and never did get the purchase that day.) Of course, this information was not revealed until sometime later. We may get lost, but we sure are encountering all the back roads of Southern Ontario. Mary and I left soon after to head home as well. I was tired and pulled over on Highway 407 for a rest. I shut my eyes for a few minutes and then continued on. I actually thought an Ontario Provincial Police patrol car would pull over and wonder what I was doing on the side of such a busy highway. It was a good rest though, and I arrived home around 5:30 p.m. and just collapsed on the couch. We had completed 15.6 km, maybe making a record for a one-day distance. A good day's work!

Hike No. 25

September 24,2004

Well, it was a warm Friday this time! The temperature was near 30°C (84°F) and we knew it. Perspiration was the name of the game. We arrived within a couple of minutes of each other in the Mono Mills area of Albion Hills. We had to wait a few minutes for the Glen Haffy Conservation Area warden to open the gate for the day. Some men were fishing at a lovely trout pond. What a lovely park—very large, picnic tables everywhere, clean washrooms. It was the beginning of three trails as well as the Bruce Trail. We were starting later than we had hoped and got under way around 9:20 a.m. under clear blue skies but warm, warm temperatures.

We went through an open parkland, descended down the escarpment, across a stream and into the woods, and eventually arrived at Highway 9. Here we walked along the shoulder of the road for a few meters and then crossed the highway and came to a babbling brook along a reservoir and up a steep hill on a bush road. When we reached the top, we walked along the edge of a field and back down to a ravine and a wide forest road. Climbing out of the valley, we came to a hardwood bush and again descended back down to the ravine. It appeared as if it was going to be one of those "up and down" days. And it was! Heading back up again, we encountered what they call switchbacks. The area was very steep, and the trail veered back and forth so you could actually get to the top. Soon we came to a clearing and a great view of the east and the southeast. We decided to have our lunch here. There was a nice bench, but it was in the sun, and at 11:30 a.m., it was getting warmer every minute, so we chose a grassy area in the shade. There was a plaque here, and we were actually at Humber Heights. This place, some 14,000 years ago, was underneath two to three meters of heavy ice. Being at such a height, it is amazing to think it was completely covered so recently, as the Ice Age had been occurring for ever so much longer. Leaving here, we hiked along the edge of an abandoned gravel pit and arrived at Mono 7th Line. We continued on to Mono 5th Sideroad. We were coming to an area that gave us some frustration, as the trail markings were very vague and very far between.

We eventually arrived at a tai chi center, and spoke to a lady there who gave us some idea of where we were. She kindly offered us a cup of green tea, but as we were beginning to run behind, we declined and continued on. We came to 5th Sideroad again and were just a few feet from Airport Road. I think some changes had been made in the route (as was sometimes the case), as our maps did not coincide with the blazes along the way. We continued walking up Airport Road, and we were passed by a number of cars.

The people were extremely friendly, or else they thought we were crazy, but they waved as they passed by. No one stopped to ask if we knew where we were going. And indeed, we were not sure. Eventually, we saw another blaze and kept on walking, hoping to come to 5th Line. (Oh, these sides and lines—what a time we had). We decided we would give Mary a call and have her come over to 4th Line and pick us up.

By now it was 2:00 p.m., and we were hot and tired to say the least. I could not get phone service down in the valley, so we walked up yet another hill, but still no service. We had nothing else to do except to start walking up 5th Line EHS (whatever that means) and phoning again once we climbed up yet another hill. It really was a lovely country road with lovely farms along the way and some very nice homes—more modest than the ones we had encountered in the Halton Hills area. Finally, climbing up a very high hill, I was able to reach Mary, who immediately drove from 4th Line EHS to pick us up. And none too soon! By now it was 2:45 p.m., and we had walked 2 km along 5th Line alone, actually making it 14.3 km. It was not as far as some hikes, but it was the up and down and the heat that made it so tiring. Mary drove us back to our cars at Glen Haffy Conservation Area, and we noticed a nice little restaurant just across the road, so we stopped and got some nourishment.

We left at 4:00 p.m. for home. Although I encountered a road closure on Airport Road and got detoured into Queen Street in mid-Toronto, I finally got onto Highway 407 and, from there on, home. It was okay except for heavy traffic coming from the city at day's end. Still it was a good day, and we were at the 274.1 km point of our hike. We are hoping for another hike on October 16 or 17. Till then, we'll keep our boots at the ready.

Hike No. 26

October 17, 2004

It was Sunday, October 17, 2004, and we sure had a change of pace weather-wise on this hike. Last hike, we had the air-conditioning on in the car, and the weather was super hot. This time we had the heat and the defroster on. So we certainly did have a variety of weather.

We arrived at approximately 9:00 a.m. as usual. Bernice had already put on her boots and rain pants due to the fact it was raining fairly steady. I donned my rain gear and boots, and Bernice finished doing the same. Well, I must say, we were a sight to behold and sure looked funny in my estimation.

Bernice Chemical Spill Hike 26 2004

Lorraine Chemical Spill Hike 26 2004

However, we were kept dry, and for a long hike, we certainly didn't want to get ourselves wet (as we previously had).

We began at 9:20 a.m. on the 5th Line, headed into the woods, and really expected to be at 4th Line in no time. However, it took us forty minutes to get to 4th Line, but it was a nice stretch. We continued on to 3rd Line where we soon turned into a gravel road that leads up to the top of the Hockley Valley Ski Resort ski tows. By now the sun had come out, and we were quite comfortable. We took a break and had a little something to eat to keep up our strength. At this point, Bernice took a picture of the view to the north, where the fall colors were just beautiful. What a lovely panoramic view! We started downhill along the side of the ski runs, across golf cart paths, and continuing with switchbacks to the bottom of the hill and a stream.

Again, we climbed back to the top of the steep incline and viewed the stunning fall colors. We passed through a pasture with a small herd of cows. All the while Bernice was hoping there wasn't a bull in the group. There wasn't, and the cows were not too interested in us. We headed to the corner of the pasture under some lovely large trees, and I think this must have been their Pooh Parlor because we really had to watch our steps. Climbing the stile, we were now on 2nd Line, and we followed it along to Dufferin Road 7, otherwise known as Hockley Road.

From 2nd Line, we entered the bush again and took the Tom East Side Trail. We came across a group of ten to twelve people out for a Sunday hike. When they saw us in our rain gear, they thought we were experts out looking for a chemical spill. We had a good laugh at that!

They took off ahead of us, and we climbed over another stile into a nice hardwood bush, a clearing, and another nice pasture with some more cows. Crossing that field, we entered another bush and walked along a portion of the Nottawasaga River. This river was about a two-foot wide stream. What a shock! We always thought the Nottawasaga River was pretty large. We crisscrossed this river over a series of bridges, and eventually the river widened to five or six feet. We stopped here to have our lunch and removed our rain jackets, hoping the rain was over for the day. Indeed, it was, except for a brief spat, which seemed more like water blowing off the trees.

We were advised to look for a deep hollow beside the trail. What they call a dry kettle was left by the glacial moraine by a melting ice block. As we progressed through a tall pine forest (which is always a lovely walk), I thought I heard something, and indeed, I did. It was my cell phone ringing. Modern life . . . technology follows you into the depths of the forest. Jim was anxious to know where we were because it was now after 2:00 p.m., and we had hoped to be finished by now.

We said we were okay and were coming along, and almost fifty minutes later, after crossing yet another lovely pasture with a beautiful eastern view, we met up with Jim, who had been waiting ever so patiently.

We found our way back to the cars with some real narrow hairpin turns (typical country roads), which did not suit Jim too well. It had been a long day, and it was now 3:00 p.m. We gave up our usual coffee break and said farewell and left for home.

Bernice's birthday was coming up soon, so I wished her a happy birthday and, of course, many more. We were hoping to get in one more hike this year, perhaps when my daughter Jennifer is home so she could join us. We are now at the 286.9 km mark.

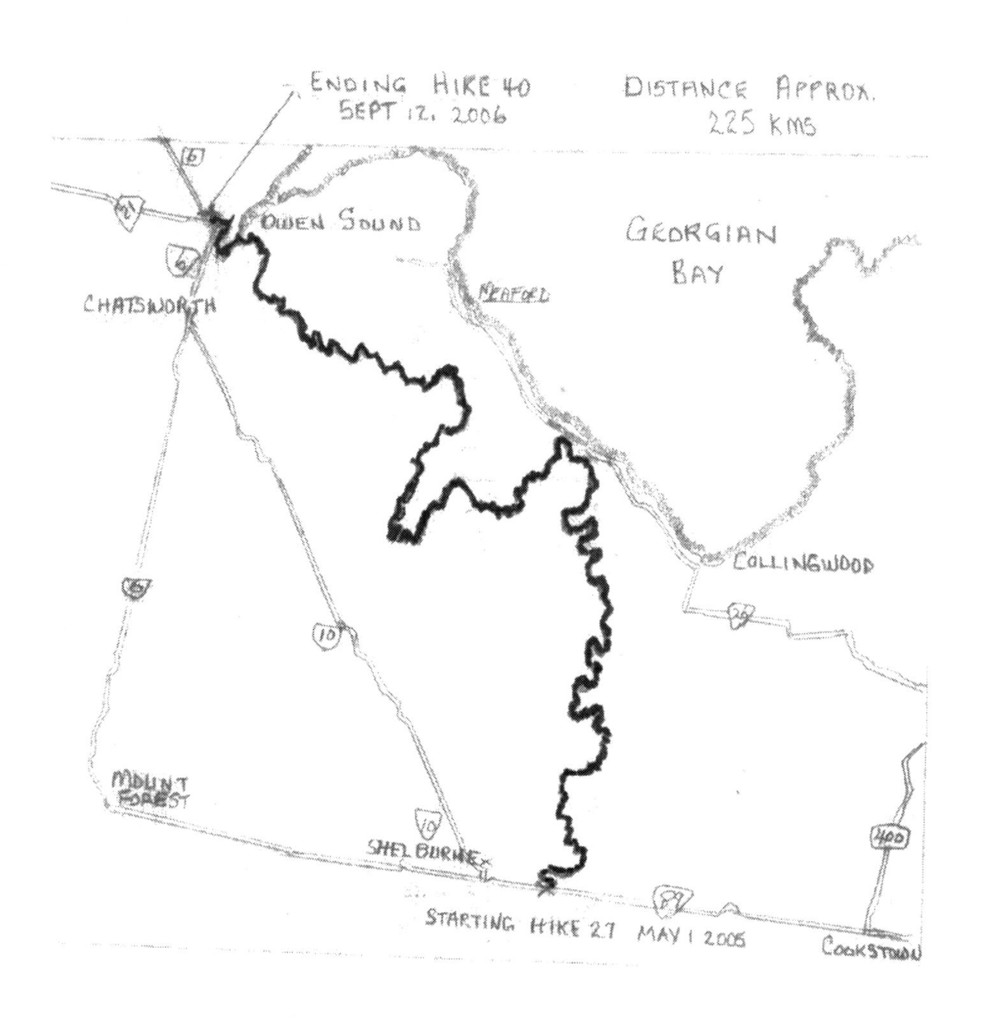

Map of Bruce Trail May 1 2005 September 2006

Hike No. 27

May 1. 2005

Well, here we are starting a new year! It was Sunday May 1, 2005. We tried to get out before, but many things seemed to hinder that plan. This day turned out to be a good one. We had best go back to the beginning.

The whole plan started when I was invited to a schoolgirl get-together in Guelph, Ontario, on a Saturday. Since I was going to be in the area, we decided to take advantage of that fact and planned for me to stay the night at Bernice's house.

We started out bright and early Sunday in the sunshine, leaving the house at 8:00 a.m. Actually, the drive to our destination was quite nice and, as Bernice said, seemed to be shorter when we traveled together. We talked all the way, and that made the time pass quickly. With one quick stop for coffee, we arrived at Dunby Road at 9:27 a.m. This was just about the time Bernice had calculated we would arrive. Good judge, eh?

After donning all our gear and checking our backpacks, we started out at 9:45 a.m. up Dunby Road and turned left onto 3rd Line, heading north. This took us to Dufferin Road 8, which we crossed and climbed over our first stile of the day. This was the end of the Caledon Hills Club.

We began a slow rise over open fields and crossed under hydro lines and came to an old cart track and the entrance to Mono Cliffs Provincial Park. To our right was a side trail looping the Southern Outlier previously mentioned on our hike no. 18 of May 28, 2004. Here we met our first adventurers of the day—a couple riding bikes and then a man with two large German shepherds. They were beautiful dogs, but we were glad their master had good control of them.

We hiked along a wide trail, which was common in a provincial park area, and this one was complete with outdoor facilities. How nice it was! However, bunnies had apparently also thought it was a good place to stop. Still, it was better than the "all outdoors." Continuing on, we stopped to look at the height of the cliffs. I They were very impressive.

Mono Cliff Prov. Park—Cliffs Hike 27 2005

The trail headed north, and we passed a pond on to 2nd Line EHS and began to climb the escarpment. We encountered a stream with a boardwalk bridge and decided to stop for a snack. After our break, we climbed over another stile and headed west again over open fields and light bush. To our surprise, we came to another stile, and we were at 25th Sideroad. It was our destination for the day, and it was only 12:00 p.m. Jim was supposed to come around 3:00 p.m. That is the difference between an easy hike and the more difficult ones we had previously experienced. We called Jim, as he was picking us up at the end of the trail, but he had already left home, so we started on to 1st Line EHS along 25th Sideroad. We called again. Jim was in Fergus, Ontario, and was surprised to hear from us so early. We headed another 400 meters up the hill. Our total for the day was 10.8 km. It was more than we had intended to hike, but we were so pleased with the easiness of the trail.

There was one item of note—the weather. Being May 1, we certainly did not expect to encounter what we did. Between sunny periods, black clouds showered us with snow-like hail, not once but four different times. It was better than rain, and all in all it was a great start to a new year of hiking. We were hoping to make it to Collingwood, Ontario, this year! Good luck to us. We will be hiking on May 15—assuming all is well.

Jim came along and picked us up, and we headed back to the starting point. Getting the car, we headed back to Bernice's where she provided us with a lovely cold supper. I called home and told Ric I would be home within a couple of hours. I left at exactly 6:00 p.m., the city hall clock ringing out the hour, and arrived in my driveway at 7:15 p.m. It was excellent traveling time. So here's to May 15.

Hike No. 28

May 15, 2005

Given the fact that we were now looking at a three-hour drive for me from Niagara Falls, I was spending the night with Bernice at her home so we could get an early start and only have an hour and a half drive from there. Still, it was a fair distance before we could begin our hike.

With all that in mind, I arrived at Bernice's at about 4:45 p.m. on Saturday, May 14, 2005. Jim had already arrived, and Mary came soon after. Bernice had prepared a lovely dinner of chicken, rice pilaf, fresh asparagus, and tomatoes. However, the best was yet to come—rhubarb pie! What can I say? It was delicious! I need not say it is my favorite. After enjoying our dinner, we spent a nice evening visiting, and at about 9:30 p.m., Mary and Jim took their leave. Bernice and I sat for a bit and then headed off to bed for a good night's sleep and, hopefully, a sunny day in the morning.

Mother Nature did accommodate us. We rose, had breakfast, and left Bernice's at 7:25 a.m., arriving at our destination at 9:00 a.m. We were off on foot soon after 9:00 a.m. on 1st Line EHS, up a little incline to a hilltop skirting fields, with a lovely panoramic view to the north and the south. The height here is almost 480 km. After crossing some fields and about three stiles, we arrived at 30th Sideroad. Here, we turned right and went north to Highway 89. We stopped here for a little break and then continued north on Centre Road, which took us about another 1.3 km to the Boyne River Side Trail. We are now in the Boyne Valley Provincial Park.

It was pleasant to hear so many birds this day, as it was a cheery and pleasant accompaniment. Climbing to a lookout, we descended along an old bush road back to 1st Line EHS. We walked up 1st Line and crossed the rushing Boyne River, which is approximately twenty feet wide and fairly deep. The trail turned back into the bush. We noticed a large sign reading Boyne River Natural Science School. The trail took us along a ravine and up a steep incline to the top of the escarpment and back down a deep descent. When we reached a dried-up streambed, we walked along it again, arriving at 1st Line EHS. Before heading up the highway, we found a nice large log and had our lunch. All the while, dark clouds came and went; however, we did not get rained on. We were happy about that.

Back on 1st Line EHS, we headed north, encountering residents driving by, of whom almost all waved a greeting. Passing lovely farmland, we saw horses, cows, and sheep on the various farms. It was nice for a couple of city girls. The horses came over to have a look at us too. Bernice is a true horse lover, having owned her own horse at one time. They may have pondered upon the strange outfits these city folk wear. Backpacks, hats, mitts, and sticks were all part of our gear. The wind was pretty brisk for the middle of May, and we both got a bit of windburn. It was better than sunburn though.

Around 1:30 p.m., we received a call from our pickup man (Jim) who informed us he was in position and awaiting our arrival. We soon met Jim (a welcome sight, as always) and proceeded back to pick up Bernice's SUV. We were extremely pleased with the hike. It had gone well, and we had made good time for 16.2 km. We got into Bernice's SUV and followed Jim to a small restaurant (Lady Jo's) near Fergus and stopped for a bit of a late lunch. We started for home and arrived at Bernice's and had a cold drink, and at precisely 5:00 p.m. (by the town clock striking the hour), I left for home, arriving at 6:30 p.m. We agreed it was a good hike, a good day, and a great way to spend a day. We planned for a May 29 hike next time and will repeat the whole thing over again, only we will have 16.3 km less to hike on *an odyssey* of the Bruce.

Hike No. 29

May 29, 2005

We started out on Saturday evening, May 28, 2005. Bernice and Jim were joining friends for dinner, so Mary and I enjoyed our favorite barbecue at Pioneer Bar-B-Q on Kitchener Highway. This place has been a favorite eatery of ours from the time we were kids, although time has really changed the landscape. It once stood at about the halfway mark between Preston (my hometown) and Kitchener (Mary's hometown now). It was out in the country. Today it is almost lost in the extensive growth of the area. However, the reputation remains. We had our barbecues, and I ordered rhubarb pie for dessert. I had to admit—Bernice's was clearly the winner. We accepted Bernice's hospitality and returned to her house and watched a movie while awaiting her return. At 10:30 p.m., Bernice arrived home, and Mary left to head to her home, and Bernice and I prepared for a good night's sleep and an early start the next day.

We did indeed get away at about 7:30 a.m. on Sunday morning as we had hoped and made good headway. There was little traffic on this early Sunday morning. We took my car this time, and Bernice seemed to enjoy not having to drive. We reached our destination at a large parking area on 1st Line EHS at about 9:00 a.m. and were off on yet another trek of the Bruce. Almost immediately, we headed into a rocky area covered with moss and ferns with some very interesting formations. Caves were dark and deep, and we had to be very cautious while walking through this area. It was very scenic though, and it was a nice start to the day. We entered a pine plantation and came out on Dufferin Road 17, which took us to a little place called Whitfield, Ontario. A lovely little church on the corner was our indicator to turn up Hurontario Street (Centre Road), and we then descended into a ravine. We followed along a little stream and arrived at River Road near Old Kilgorie School, which dated back to 1909. It is now someone's residence.

On River Road, we crossed over Pine River and entered back into the bush and followed the river to the remains of the Dufferin Light and Power Generating Company building. This electrical company supplied the hydro to the surrounding area back in the early days of the century.

Pine River Dufferin Power Generating Hike 29, 2005

We hiked back up the hill and eventually back to River Road. We followed a bush track that took us up past Horning's Mills Fishing and Game Preserve. This brought back many memories for us. A dear friend of my husband, Rip Painting, had owned the fish hatchery at Horning's Mills, Ontario, back in the late '50s. We had spent many a good time there in days gone by.

The next part of the trail really tested our endurance, as it was a series of steps up the trail. Just when we thought we had reached a plateau, we turned, and there were another twenty-five to thirty steps more. Upon reaching the top, to our right was a lookout point showing the Pine River Provincial Fishing Area. It was quite a nice view from this vantage point. Back to the main trail, we arrived at 15 Sideroad, and crossing this, we continued up 1st Line WHS to 20 Sideroad. All day, clouds had come and gone many times, but dark gray clouds had been to the east and with the wind picking up and thunder off in the distance, we were preparing for rain. We had stopped along Pine River for a break and had our lunch also once we reached the top of the steps. We knew we were on the last lap. The rain started. It was actually hail in the beginning, and we called our pickup person (Mary this time) ahead, and she quickly came to our rescue. What would we have done without our rescuers? We only had about a ten-minute walk (or less) but chose to forego that section and get out of the rain. We drove back to our car and followed Mary back to Fergus, Ontario, where we stopped for something to eat. The food in the small deli with eight to ten tables was great. We visited for a bit and decided to head on home, as I still had to drive back to Niagara Falls. We were hoping for hike no. 30 by mid-June and may go midweek, as we had found a back-road route with little traffic. Leaving Bernice's at 6:30 p.m., I arrived home at around 7:45 p.m. We had completed 13 km and a successful day.

Hike No. 30

June 22, 2005

This was the perfect day weather-wise. Otherwise, it was not so perfect! It was Wednesday, June 22, 2005. Jim was kind enough to drive us up this time. However, for some reason, we had trouble finding our starting place. We finally got going around 9:45 a.m., with Jim wishing us luck. He drove off to have a golf game at the Shelburne Golf and Country Club, and we struck out across a small field and into a bush and a steep decline. The trail was filled with rocks and many, many leaves. We cautiously proceeded to the bottom of the valley, encountering many little rivulets and streams and a very damp trail. We crossed a small bridge and exited on Centre Road.

The weather was just right for a hike or a golf game, so we all started with high hopes. We followed the road for a bit and then dropped down again and then started up the original Hurontario Street road allowance. This was only a narrow trail, probably used by horse and buggies originally. We then continued along some private land to Dufferin Road 21 at Black Bank. Turning west, we were to go about 150 meters and then turn across a hay field into a pine plantation. After hiking six hundred to seven hundred meters, we ended back at Centre Road. So according to the map, this would take us to 30 Sideroad, which it did. We reread our map and the write-up and somehow missed our turn into the field. Probably too busy talking! Rather than travel back, we just continued on up Centre Road. By this time, it was 12:30 p.m., so we stopped for our lunch. We stopped under some lovely shade trees and enjoyed some veggies and fruit and rested for a while and began hiking again at around 12:45 p.m.

The scenery was great, and the weather, we commented again, couldn't have been nicer, so although we had missed part of the trail, we were really enjoying our hike. We crossed 30 Sideroad and started up a long hill and very soon arrived at Lavender. This was a hamlet of five houses and one church at the intersection of Centre Road and Baseline. Here, there was a Bruce Trail sign prominently displayed on a hydro pole, showing us the way up Baseline, a distance of 625 km to our next turn into some cedars and mixed hardwood bush. Well, we walked and we walked and never did find any more trail blazes, and Bernice finally thought that perhaps our maps were outdated and some changes had been made, and that is why we couldn't find the trail. Dahhh! We decided this must be the case, but it did not rectify the situation we found ourselves in.

We were now several kilometers up the road at the intersection of Mulmar Township Line and 2nd Line West (wherever that was). We were sitting in the corner, deciding what to do, when we saw a white car coming along in the distance. I decided I would stop the car when it slowed for the corner and ask *the question*—where were we? However, when the white car arrived at the corner, it was an Ontario Provincial Police car, and the officers did the questioning. "What are you doing here?" It became quite hilarious. While Bernice chatted with one of the officers who had his comprehensive map laid out on the trunk of the car and was trying to show her where we were, I chatted with the officer in the car, explaining how we had been hiking and looking for the blazes on the Bruce Trail and couldn't find any and had actually thought of starting a fire so we could see a blaze. They were very kind and accepted quaint humor and kidded us about their being out on the back roads looking for some suspicious persons carrying walking sticks. After some deliberation, we were able to call Jim and advise him where we were. They went on their way (probably shaking their heads in disbelief), and soon our knight in shining SUV arrived to help the fair maidens in distress—once again!

Fortunately, all was not lost. Jim had enjoyed a good day with some people from the golf club, and so we were happy about that. We drove to Shelburne, had a bite of lunch, and then drove home to Jim's place where we picked up Bernice's car, thanked Jim again for his patience and understanding of two lost souls, and headed on to Bernice's house.

We did a little side trip to pay a visit to Dave's resting place. Bernice's husband had passed away a few years earlier. He had been a wonderful husband and a dear friend of my husband and myself. An interesting note was that I had introduced Bernice and Dave many years before, and Bernice had introduced my husband and me a few years later. So we had all been friends for a many long years. We sat by a fountain in downtown Cambridge, had coffee, and reflected on the good times we had shared over the years. Once again, at six bells, I left for home after thanking Bernice, knowing there would be lots of hikes to come and perhaps one in the next two to three weeks, depending on the heat of the summer.

Hike No. 31

July 10, 2005

This hike began with me arriving at Bernice's home on Saturday, July 9, 2005, just around suppertime. We decided to go for a hamburger and fries at a place in Cambridge, which was located along the banks of the Grand River. After we ate, we walked along the river and enjoyed a lovely summer evening. Returning home, we watched a little news and the Weather Channel to check on the next day's prediction. We decided to turn in earlier than usual in hopes of rising bright-eyed and bushy tailed for the next day's hike.

We arose at 6:30 a.m. on the tenth and had our usual light fare for breakfast and picked up Jim at Preston at around 7:30 a.m. to start the day. Jim drove, and we made good time, stopping for coffee at a little deli on the way, and we arrived at Dunedin Road (also known as Simcoe County Road 9) and Concession 10. This stretch was very well marked. We followed the brow of the escarpment up and over stiles to the 9-10 Sideroad. Along the top of the escarpment, we saw what was described as drumlins. These are piles of rock shifted by the Ice Age into twenty—or thirty-foot piles that look like someone had stacked them all very neatly.

As it turned out, it was a very warm day, and we were tiring quickly. When we came to Concession 10 again, we called our ever-faithful driver to come, as we were not willing to continue in the midday heat. As luck would have it, Jim was just coming down the road and met us within a couple of minutes. He was a welcome sight.

We stopped on the way back for a snack at the deli and then continued on home. I picked my things up at Bernice's and was soon on my way home. We were somewhat disappointed about only completing 10.3 km. It is a long way to drive for such a short hike. We will wait for cooler weather before hiking again. We would be waiting for that time anxiously, as we had hoped to get out every other week or so. It seems to be slow progress, but in fact, we were doing very well.

Hike No. 32

September 6, 2005

We were not looking forward to this hike. After a summer of excessively high temperatures and humidity, we were dreading that even though it was September, we would be facing a hot and humid trip. However, Mother Nature smiled on us; and as it turned out, it was one of the better hikes we had so far encountered. Things seem to work out. Let me fill you in!

I arrived at Bernice's on Monday evening, September 5, 2005, just in time for dinner, which was delicious. We spent some time mapping out the next day's hike. We called Mary to arrange our timing for the next day, as we were planning on staying overnight at Mary's sister's home in Collingwood, conveniently located near the Bruce Trail, and Mary was driving us on this trip.

Up early, we left Bernice's and hit early morning traffic and arrived at Mary's nearly a half hour late at 8:30 a.m. We transferred all of our gear to Mary's car and started off on a lovely late summer day. We stopped for a coffee but didn't hesitate to get on the road again fairly quickly. We arrived at our destination at 10:45 a.m., and Mary dropped us at the side of the road on Concession 10 and 12-13 Sideroad. Mary continued on to her sister Ida's home, where she planned to wait for us to call when we were finished with our hike.

The trail headed up the road a bit and then into a field and through a treed, rocky area, which again reminded us of the Niagara area. The trail reached the top of the escarpment, and we followed along the escarpment. The trail was well marked and easy to follow where we finally rejoined the Nottawasaga side trail. We hiked along a cart track on the Devil's Glen Ski Club property and continued to 15-16 Sideroad. Here, we stopped for lunch. What a beautiful day. It was such a pleasure being out in the country, in the fresh air with a lovely breeze and lots of sun, not too hot, just comfortable.

We next arrived at a pine plantation, which was so quiet and peaceful, and then arrived at the top of a ski slope. We came to a bridge that crossed the Mad River 150 meters down the slope. It was a sparkling stream, and the water was so inviting that we found a rock, took off our hiking boots, and paddled our feet in the cool water. Beautiful trees hung over the stream, giving us nice shade from the sun. What a lovely few minutes it was. We decided then and there that being able to hike at our own pace and not have to worry that someone was patiently waiting at the other end for us was a decidedly better plan. It seemed we were much more relaxed and not so tired because we were taking our time, taking in more of the scenery, and stopping frequently to rest and view the area.

Following along the Mad River for some six hundred meters, we gradually turned away and began a long steep ascent to the top of the escarpment. This was a combination of stretches of wooden steps and stretches of just trail covering 130 steps in all. It took us a few stops along this steep incline to reach the top, which brought us to the Devils' Glen Provincial Park.

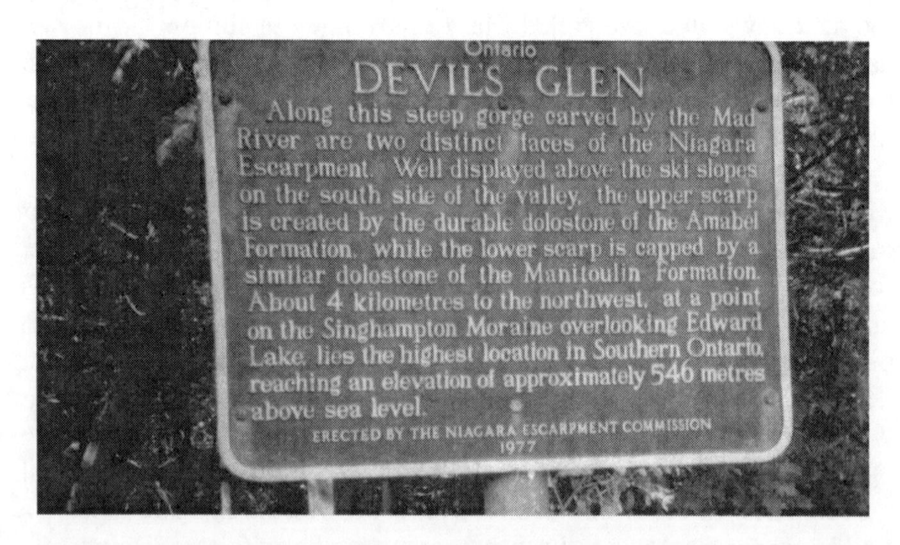

Plaque Depicting Devil's Glen Hike 32 2005

We ended our hike for the day and phoned Mary.

Both Mary and Ida came along soon after, and we arrived at Ida's at around 4:00 p.m. It was nice to see Ida again, as the last time had been a few years before at a reunion in Preston. We were refreshed by having a nice shower and sitting outside before leaving for Ida's daughter's restaurant in Collingwood. We enjoyed a delicious dinner and went back to Ida's and sat outside at the picnic bench in the backyard and planned our route for the next day. We were soon ready for bed, and I think all of us must have been quite tired. We turned in at around 9:30 p.m., and none of us awakened until 6:00 a.m. or 6:30 a.m. It was a great night's sleep, and after a lovely breakfast prepared by Ida, we got ready for our day's hike.

Hike No. 33

September 7, 2005

We had finished at 21-22 Sideroad and Concession 10 on Tuesday, so this Wednesday, September 7 we began again when Mary dropped us off at 9:00 a.m. Another lovely hike stretched before us, and we felt surprisingly well considering we had hiked 13.8 km the previous day. After about seven hundred meters, we turned into a field skirting along a hedgerow and into a maple forest and continued along the escarpment edge. We came to a large field with one lone maple tree in the middle. It was quite a lovely sight. Passing the maple, we continued north to a field, turned right, and descended along a cedar rail fence to 26-27 (Lobsinger) Sideroad. We stopped for a break and sat on a little wooden walkway over a small stream. It was now 10:00 a.m. We were doing quite well, so we crossed the road, continuing north along the escarpment to a mature forest, and stopped for our lunch on the Nottawasaga-Osprey Townline.

We followed this road, and then the trail took us back to the edge of the escarpment where we had to descend quite steeply down through crevices in the rocks and continue to the base. At the top, there was the standing rock lookout, but with all the foliage, the view was still pretty well hidden.

At the base, we crossed a stream, continued along a fence line, and came to 30-31 Sideroad. We had completed 10.1 km for a total of 23.9 km in two days. Not too bad for a couple of senior ladies!

When we arrived at 30-31 Sideroad, we phoned Mary, and she and Ida were at Tim Horton's about to have lunch. It was 12:30 p.m. We had made better time than we had anticipated. Mary took Ida home and came and picked us up, and we started back home again. Since Mary had been cheated out of her lunch, we stopped at the deli again and had a bite to eat and then were on our way home. We arrived at Mary's around 4:00 p.m., and as I hadn't seen her new condo, she took us on a tour. It is a very nice place, and Mary seems very happy and comfortable there.

We bid our farewells and hoped to do the same thing again within a couple of weeks. We were hoping our plan would work out. At Bernice's I gathered the rest of my belongings and headed back to the falls, arriving home at 7:15 p.m.

They had been quite eventful days, and we were quite pleased with the outcome. A good bit of the trail had been completed, and the weather had cooperated beautifully. It had been nice to visit with Mary and Ida, who had taken in the weary hikers and provided food and sustenance. We were invited to stay again, and as we planned to come back soon, we offered our appreciation and stated we would gratefully accept the offer.

Hike No. 34

September 27, 2005

Monday, September 26, I arrived at Bernice's right on time at 5:15 p.m., and as usual, Bernice had a tasty dinner awaiting me. After dinner, amid much laughter at our ineptitude, we finally managed to plan our way to and from our pickup and finish areas. With Ontario road maps and Bruce Trail maps, it can get rather confusing, especially when we also had updates to the Bruce to consider. Anyway, as with any trip, the planning can be almost as much fun as the trip itself. We just hoped we would be able to follow our plans and maps the next day without getting lost. In fact, we had Ida and her son Larry looking at maps on Tuesday morning after we arrived at Ida's, and it was very amusing trying to get all of us on the same page (so to speak).

Alas, we finally agreed on the day's route and stop-and-go locations, and after a lovely breakfast provided again by Ida, we gathered our gear for the day and left the rest at Ida's and set out for day one, hike no. 34, and the best possible weather to boot. We followed Larry and Ida in their car to the end part of our trail for the day, which was 2nd Line and New Mountain Road or Grey County Road 19. It is interesting that in the country, it appears that a number of the roads have an area road name and a county road name. This is just to confuse novice hikers and poor map readers. We left our car there, and Larry and Ida drove us back to 30-31 Sideroad to begin another day of hiking the Bruce. Donning our boots and backpacks, with hiking sticks in hand and with enthusiasm abounding, we bid Larry and Ida farewell.

It was 10:30 a.m., 13°C (56°F), and a perfect day for hiking. Nice temperature, a slight breeze, and no humidity. Who could ask for anything more? We headed down an unopened road allowance through some wet areas with wooden walkways and reached the Pretty River. We followed the bank of the river, which was very scenic, with lovely bubbling water and low-hanging trees along the riverbank, to Grey County Road 31. We encountered a lot of milkweed and crab apple trees along the way. We climbed a steep hill through scrubby areas with a view of the Pretty River Valley. It was now 11:45 a.m.

From there we entered a transition forest, descended again through a cedar forest—very narrow and dark and later we encountered scrubby patches—and were back at Grey County Road 31. We crossed over a stream and bridge and kept crossing the stream, climbing gradually. We stopped for lunch at 1:00 p.m. As we were eating, a loud sound, like that of a tree falling or a very large branch breaking, interrupted our peaceful repast. We hoped it was simply that and not a bear lunging through the bush. I guess we were spooked because as we hiked along the trail, at one point, we gasped for a moment, as gazing out at us from the base of a tree was what we took to be a wolf. Thankfully it was just the shape of the tree and the other pieces of wood surrounding it that made it appear as it did. The really amazing thing about this part of the trail, however, was that we were now at the highest point of the Bruce Trail at 546 meters.

Highest Point on Bruce Trail 546m Hike 34 2005

We were really getting up in the world! Bernice captured a lovely scenic view from the top of the escarpment.

We proceeded to a pine plantation and then through maple woods to the Gibraltar Sideroad. This was a very rocky area with granite boulders, which are called erratics. This is because the rocks were moved from another place by the glaciers and were just left there after the ice melted. It is so interesting to see what Mother Nature has done so many thousands or even millions of years ago. Our time on this earth is so infinitesimal. If you want to put life into perspective, try hiking some of the trails of our province.

We were in the Petun Conservation Area, where there is a Petun Indian Cemetery. The Petun Indians lived in this area in the mid-1600s. Seneca Indians killed most of them, and the rest fled to Southern Ontario and the northern states.

We eventually came to 2nd Line, and a lady was just coming by, so we asked her if there was a parking lot nearby, and she said there was one just up the road to our left and we should just keep going and we won't miss it. So we hiked up the gravel road, up a hill, around a bend, up another hill, and came to another road and a parking lot. However, it was not the parking lot we were looking for. The side road crossing 2nd Line was not marked, so we, *again*, had no idea where we were. Doesn't this just happen too often? It was, however, amusing because while we were trying to decide what to do, a chap came out of the woods, from a side trail, and offered to drive us back to where we had come from and back down to Grey County Road 19, where we were supposed to be. Doesn't this just happen too often as well? That some good fellow comes along and saves the day for us? Whatever the reason, we certainly appreciate it. We thanked the chap profusely and got into our car and found our way back to Ida's.

We went to the pub for dinner and then back to Ida's for an early bed. What a day! We had hiked almost 14 km (maybe more with our diversion). We were still making good headway for a couple of old girls.

Hike No. 35

September 28, 2005

Another day, September 28, 2005. Bernice and I arose and prepared for another hike. As Ida prepared breakfast for us, we gathered up our suitcases, dressed in our hiking gear, and loaded the car. We planned to leave for home immediately upon completion of the day's hike. We followed Larry up the escarpment, a lovely drive, and arrived at the very top of the escarpment overlooking Georgian Bay and Collingwood. It was a picture-perfect view. Larry drove back to the beginning of our day's hike at 2nd Line and 19 County Road. We bid farewell to Ida and Larry and thanked them again for their map and their hospitality. It was 9:30 a.m.

We immediately entered into a wooded area and climbed up and then back down to the Pretty River. On the up climb, we encountered a chap on a dirt bike coming down, and later, when we crossed 3rd Line, he was heading back down the road, having done a complete turn.

As we hiked along the road allowance, which skirted the Blue Mountain ski slopes, we encountered three hikers lunching on the picnic tables. It was rather unusual to meet other hikers along the way. We continued on and came to a ski-tow tractor with a wagon with six or seven rows of seats. It seemed like the perfect place to take a rest and have a snack. We were having difficulty with our location, as the trail map had changed. Bernice was perusing it once again (for about the fortieth time), and I was struck with a bout of laughter, commenting that she should have it memorized by now. I'm sure these moments of minor hysteria were good. We may have otherwise long ago given up. Anyway, being the good sport that she was, we enjoyed the moment and went on and finally arrived at the top of the escarpment again. As we continued on to the road, we passed old army vehicles rusting away in the field. We thought they too may have been used as ski-tow vehicles but had seen better days. We hiked along Scenic Caves Road and continued along the top of the escarpment. These scenic caves are deep crevices that people, who do not suffer from claustrophobia, can enter and edge through and exit several feet later. The trail itself at this point was so close to the edge that it was no longer used. So down the road we proceeded about 1 km and stopped at the top of the ski trail and ate our lunch while looking at the wonderful view of Georgian Bay and Collingwood.

Rounding the bend, we passed through Swiss Meadows Subdivision, a touch of suburbia, and arrived at Maple Lane and our car. We were tired but had made good time, as it was only 12:30 p.m. We took some pictures of the stunning views, got into the car, and found our way back through Collingwood and homeward. We had noticed on the way up the hydro wind turbines that had been erected since our previous trip in July. There seemed to be about fifteen or more and they were obviously still building more as attested to by the sky-high cranes dotting the landscape.

We arrived home at about 3:45 p.m., and while Bernice checked her phone messages, I took a small catnap. Feeling somewhat refreshed, I packed up and headed on home, arriving at around 7:15 p.m. It had been another long and eventful day, and we had completed 10.3 km. We were now past the halfway mark. We hoped for another hike in October.

HIKE NO. 36

November 8, 2005

This was going to be our last hike of 2005, and we really lucked out with the weather, the trail, etc.

I arrived at Bernice's on Monday afternoon, November 7, around 7:30 p.m. We checked out the maps from start to finish and relaxed before turning in for a good night's sleep. Actually, the anticipation was not conducive to a good rest, and so Bernice arose shortly after 5:00 a.m., and I was awake not too much later. We breakfasted while watching the morning news and weather and were happy to see a fairly good weather pattern developing for the day. Anything but rain!

We arrived at Jim's at 6:45 a.m. and were all ready to leave right at 7:00 a.m. It is always pleasant when someone else can drive. It was a beautiful morning, and we enjoyed the drive and, after some slight detours, arrived at the parking area and donned our gear and readied ourselves for the day's hike. Jim, after receiving the day's instructions, left to continue on to Owen Sound, where he was going to lunch with his cousin. Later we were pleased to hear that Jim's cousin and his wife invited Bernice and I to a meal when we're again hiking in the area. We are surely hoping to take advantage of such a lovely invitation.

We were ready to go at 10:00 a.m. sharp, so we took the road allowance near Sideroad 22B and headed into Beaver Valley. We opted to take the Siegerman Side Trail, which takes a scenic route, and indeed it did. We stopped for the view at 10:45 a.m. We commented on the trail, which was very well kept and very well marked. It helped to make good time on the trail. We continued down the valley, twice crossing a very bubbly, rocky stream. We did so with some trepidation, not wanting to end up in the water. This was a place where our hiking sticks were very valuable in balancing us over troubled waters. We were now at 3rd Line. This was also a road allowance and was easily traveled. We stopped at the brow of the hill and had some lunch, and Bernice Band-Aided her feet, which were beginning to blister. We basked in the lovely noon day sun and enjoyed the beautiful day it had turned out to be. Unfortunately, a lot of the fall colors were gone. Still, it was lovely to be out on such a gorgeous day, especially knowing there would not be too many more days like this in 2005. Winter would soon be laying down her snowy blanket.

We realized that being in the valley area and bear country, we should be prepared, so we hung our bear bells on the outside of our backpacks and jingled on our way. The bear bells are similar to ordinary jingle bells, only about three or four times larger. In bear country, in case a bear doesn't know you are visiting his neighborhood, these bells will let him know, and he, hopefully, makes himself scarce.

We continued up 3rd Line, crossing 25 Sideroad, and came to historic Old Mail Road and on to Grey County Road 40. Old Mail Road, established in 1840, probably followed an old Indian trail. It was the first road in Grey County. We stopped at this juncture for another break. Following along the road for about 500 meters we turned on to private land.

Thanks to many private landowners, Bruce Trail hikers are afforded areas to hike, which are otherwise unavailable. The land became rockier, and climbing the escarpment again had us comparing it to Niagara. We passed through a pine plantation and then entered a forest with deep crevices in the rock. The trail actually passed right through a crevice, which was about fifteen to twenty feet deep.

This was not a popular place for Bernice to be, and although it only took us three or four minutes to hike through, it was too long for her. The Bruce Trail notes mention "Hart's Tongue Fern" in this area, and indeed we saw a good amount of it. It is quite different from the other ferns we saw growing along the way. It reminded us of a more rubbery type of leaf. Very nice though.

We had planned to take another break, but from our lofty perch, we could see Jim's SUV parked down County Road 7, so we phoned him and said we wouldn't be much longer. We estimated maybe a half an hour, but to our surprise, within ten to fifteen minutes, we had emerged from the trees, and we waved and waved, thinking Jim would see us. He didn't, so we phoned again and alerted him to our presence. He still couldn't see us but drove up the road, and we climbed down the hill to the highway, and it was exactly 3:00 p.m. What a day! We had a terrific hike, Jim had a good visit with his cousin, and as we made our way back home, we decided to stop for some food. Bernice and Jim had been to a lovely restaurant in Elora, so we stopped there and indeed had a nice dinner and a drink and a toast to another successful hike and another year of our Bruce Trail odyssey. We arrived back at Bernice's around 6:30 p.m., put our feet up, and recounted the day's events. We managed to stay awake for a little TV but soon went off to bed for a good night's sleep. Sleeping in a little, we had a leisurely breakfast, and I headed up to Kitchener for a visit with my daughter Jennifer, after which I picked up my grandson at the Hamilton Airport on my way back to Niagara. Bernice was going out to lunch with friends and dinner with Jim (not much cooking going on in the Scott house these days).

It was another year ending our hikes. However, we are making progress, albeit slower than most folks would. Come 2006, we hope to get to Owen Sound in the spring and maybe a start toward Wiarton. In spite of delays, getting lost, and many other events, which deterred us and slowed our progress in achieving our objective, we were happy with our efforts; and hopefully, we will continue in good health. Till next time, adieu . . .

Hike No. 37

May 7, 2006

This is the first hike of 2006 and got off to a wonderful start. I arrived at Bernice's around 5:00 p.m. on Saturday, May 6, and Mary arrived just a few minutes later. We brought each other up to date on activities since our last get-together back in November of 2005. (Actually, we had met for a quick lunch and a visit late in February in Burlington, but it had seemed like a long time since we had a good chance to chat. Bernice and Mary had a glass of wine, and I had a lovely Green Apple Twist, which I had enjoyed when Carrie, my daughter, visited from Victoria BC in April.)

Bernice served up a delicious dinner of sole (while I did my rendition of "O Sole Mio") with rice and mushrooms and a new delicious dish of black-eyed peas (brought from her recent holiday in San Miguel, Portugal). For dessert, Bernice made my favorite, rhubarb pie, and it was so delicious. We tidied up and watched the movie *Mrs. Henderson Presents* with Dame Judy Dench. It was a riot. Mary had already seen it, but from her reaction, I believe she enjoyed it just as much the second time. We had enjoyed a lovely evening, and after Mary left for home, we quickly headed off to bed for a good night's sleep, preparing for our first hike of year 2006. According to our original schedule, we should be finishing this year. But that was surely not possible.

Sunday morning, May 7, came early at 5:30 a.m. We had a quick breakfast and left for Jim's, as he was once again being a fine gentleman and driving us to our designated starting point. It was 6:45 a.m., and he was ready, and so we left on a rather chilly, cloudy morning. But it was a lovely drive, and as usual, we stopped in Durham for coffee. We arrived at our destination at 9:20 a.m. and were ready to start at 9:30 a.m. We had headbands and gloves on, as well as winter jackets, and actually still had these on when we finished the hike. It was cold for May.

We started at Grey County Road 7 and headed into a rather rocky area and through the Grey Conservation Area. It became a rather easy hike, and we made good time in the conservation area, even though we chatted and marveled at the abundance of trilliums, violets, and some small yellow flowers that we could not identify, and an occasional Jack-in-the-Pulpit. I don't believe, in my entire life, I have seen so many trilliums at once. Being Ontario's flower, it is always great to see them. The trail was nearly overrun with them. What a sight!

We followed the escarpment through bush and fields and came to an area near 7th Line that had deep crevices and, at that point, saw the walking fern referred to in the Bruce Trail guide book. The ferns seem to just grow out of the rock and travel down the side of the rock face. We saw quite a few, as there were numerous deep (and, in some places, very wide) crevices.

Trees Clinging to Rocks Hike 37 2006

It continues to amaze me how the ice from the Ice Age had the power to move these immense pieces of rock. We also saw huge rocks the size of round summer picnic tables dotting the landscape here and there, as if they had just been dropped from above.

We crossed Anthea's Waterfall (named by her father, a past president of the Bruce Trail Association). It was at the point we encountered a group of six hikers from the Kitchener area. We let them go ahead and soon came to another little creek with a log bridge over it, where we stopped for our lunch. We rested our bods for about twenty minutes and then continued on. We came out of the woods at the Blantyre Community Hall on Grey County Road 12. Crossing the road, we hiked down a farmer's lane through an open field and back into the bush. Jim called, and we met him a few minutes later at the 11th Line. It was about 2:15 p.m.

Because of the easy terrain and the coolness of the day, we felt we could have hiked another hour, but we were happy to sit down and be chauffeured to a nice restaurant for an early dinner.

For dinner we agreed to drive back to Elora to the Gorge restaurant where we had eaten last fall on our last hike of the year. The Gorge is named after a limestone canyon with caves and waterfalls that is part of the Grand River, which flows from just below Georgian Bay, 290 km to the mouth at Lake Erie, where the waters flow over Niagara Falls into Lake Ontario and down the St. Lawrence River to the Atlantic Ocean. The Elora Gorge is a beautiful scenic area. I had visited the area many times as a youngster.

We enjoyed our dinner and arrived back at Jim's around 6:15 p.m. We thanked him for his good deed for the day and drove back to Bernice's for a quiet evening and an early bed. We had completed 12.1 km.

Monday morning, Bernice was up a bit before me, but we had our tea and coffee and checked our maps for the next hike. We plan to do that around the May 18, if all goes as planned. We hope to get at least two more hikes in before the heat of summer. If we do, we will be close to Owen Sound. So keep the fingers crossed for good luck. Till next time . . .

Hike No. 38

May 25, 2006

We were going to try for the eighteenth. However, the heat was too much, so we waited for the holiday of May 24 (the Queen's birthday) and had a really good day. As usual, I arrived at Bernice's around suppertime (how convenient is that?), and she fed me a good dinner as usual, which was cannelloni and salad. We watched a little TV and got off to bed in time for a good night's rest.

Wednesday, the twenty-fifth, began at 5:30 a.m., and we managed to get to Jim's by 7:00 a.m. He was ready and waiting. It was a lovely sunny morning, and we had a pleasant drive to our destination, stopping for our usual coffee break on the way.

We began at 10:00 a.m. sharp at the Vincent-Sydenham Townline, where the trail turns into a field, past an old barn and into the woods. As we were preparing for the hike, a man came along in his car, with his dog (a springer spaniel, which was like Queenie, the dog I had as a child) and asked us some questions about our hiking and said he lived nearby on a farm and told us to drop in anytime. He gave us a sunny farewell, as did Jim, and so we were off! Country folk seem to exude friendliness. How nice it is!

It started out as a fairly pleasant hike—weather just right—and we spent some of the time in the woods. However, we crossed a number of fields that had been freshly plowed and were lumpy and bumpy and very difficult to hike over. I think we crossed about six fields, which made for some pretty sore feet and ankles at the end of the day.

We crossed Grey County Road 29 and went over a stile along a path, which followed the road, and again past the ruins of an old barn. The landscapes are dotted with decaying old barns and driving sheds, scenes from another era. It seems sad. We soon arrived at Walters Creek (which Jane Painting had asked about the last time I had talked to her). It seemed her husband Rip Painting's dad had ministered at the church at Walter's Creek many years before, and Rip had gone with him on several occasions. We actually did not see the church but crossed the creek over a nice wide wooden bridge and took this time to sit down and dabble our feet in the fresh cool water. We had a bit of lunch and enjoyed our usual twenty-minute break.

At one point, the trail followed the road and took us up a long hill in the blazing noonday sun, and it was very, very hot. However, soon after we turned back into the woods and during the whole hike, we had a nice soft summer breeze reminding me of a lovely song from back in the fifties.

After crossing the cultivated fields, and complaining about our aching arches, we arrived at a magnificent view of the Bighead Valley. The view of the valley was lovely, to say the least. We turned right on to 4th Concession and hiked up the road to where the trail turned into a farmer's lane and on up the escarpment.

We had hoped to get to get to Sideroad 3 near 6th Concession where Jim was waiting for us in the parking area, but we felt we had just about used up all of our capacity and sat down about 3 km short of our goal. We called our ever-faithful and skilled driver to come to our aid, and he managed all the steep and curvy hills (something he did not really care to travel) to pick up a pair of weary hikers. After a nice drive back to Fergus and finding us a lovely place to eat, we relaxed and enjoyed a very nice supper. We arrived back in Cambridge round 6:30 p.m., but this time we really didn't care what time it was. It was just good to be back at Bernice's for a quiet evening and a very early bed.

Up again early the next morning, I left for home around 9:30 a.m., and Bernice prepared for a luncheon she was going to. We hoped for one more hike before the sweltering weather of summer was upon us. Bernice's grandchildren from Alabama would be visiting in the next while, so we would try for another hike after their visit. We had completed approximately 9.6 km—not what we had hoped for, but we had not anticipated six fields of freshly plowed earth either. We do not weather the wear and tear like we once would have. However, we were trying to "suck it up" and "git 'er dun" slowly but surely! Hurray for us!

Hike No. 39

June 11, 2006

Well, Mother Nature smiled on us and delivered the perfect hiking day on Sunday, June 11, 2006. Checking the long-range weather forecast, Bernice called me midweek and suggested we try for Sunday, the eleventh, as the weather certainly looked favorable at that time. So planning began, and on Saturday, as usual, I arrived at Bernice's just past 5:00 p.m. and was pleased to find Jim had offered to treat us to supper at the Pioneer Bar-B-Q, a favorite place of mine. It is a place located on the highway between Preston (now Cambridge) and Kitchener and has been there since I was a little girl and probably much longer (if possible). We enjoyed barbecues and fries, and Jim had rhubarb pie (another rhubarb pie lover). I declined only because I had brought along a pecan pie (Bernice's favorite pie). We decided to wait until later for that treat. We dropped Jim at home, and we headed on to Bernice's and had our tea and pie (pretty good . . .) and did some preparing for the next day.

Arising at our usual time, we arrived at Jim's at 7:00 a.m., and with Bernice driving, me in the front, and Jim relaxing (at least he wasn't a backseat driver) in the back, we started out our day. It was a perfect day, as I said before, and we were so pleased that it was. We made our usual coffee break stop in Durham and arrived at the start-off mark at 10:00 a.m. We actually started at 9:45 a.m., but we dropped Jim off at a local golf course for a, hopefully, good game. (Sadly, we later found out, it wasn't a good day of golf for Jim and the clubs are up for sale—any buyers?).

Bernice had just purchased the updated Bruce Trail map, so we started out at 4th Concession, where we had stopped last time. The trail headed straight up to the escarpment brow through a wooded area, and then some fields (not plowed, thank goodness), to arrive, after climbing a stile, at Sideroad 3. This took us one hour. We continued through some swampy areas with a number of wooden walkways, came out onto a side road, and found ourselves rather lost. We kept to the road, heading up to a crossroads, and stopped to have a lunch and ponder our dilemma. We sat under the shade of some evergreen trees on the top of a hill and enjoyed a few minutes of the usual country peace and quiet. It certainly helps to restore the soul.

While we were hiking through Grey Sable Conservation Area earlier, we had passed a chap horseback riding. There were numerous trails for cross-country skiing and snowmobiling, as well as the hiking trails. I guess it was in this maze of trails, while we were busy chatting, that we missed a turn; but as it turned out, we were glad we did, as we encountered some interesting people and an interesting situation.

When we reached the top of the hill and stopped, wondering what to do, four fellows in an Argo eight-wheeler came up the dirt road across the highway from us. We tried to wave them down, hoping for some information on where we were, and they happily waved back. Not until we shouted and waved frantically did they stop and wait for us to catch up so we could ask (again, the frequently asked question) where we were. I guess four guys out for a Sunday ride through the swamp in their Argo, having a relaxing day, didn't expect to encounter the likes of us. However, gentlemen that they were, they listened to our plight and offered to give us a ride up to the next concession. We were two concessions from our destination, but they were turning off on the next one. We gratefully took them up on their offer, jumped into the eight-wheeler, and had a jolly good ride up the highway. We were offered a cold drink. We declined, but we managed to get their names but forgot to get a picture. However, hats off to Mike, Wayne, DJ, and Al for the lift and the directions. We certainly appreciated it.

We bid farewell and hiked one concession and on to Derry Road (also called Grey County Road 18). One thing we learned from hiking the Bruce Trail is that it seems every road has two names, which is very confusing for two city girls. From there it was 5.5 km to our destination at the crossroads of Highway 6 and Concession 10, where we were to meet Jim. Hiking up the road, we realized why the Trail was wisely routed through the countryside. It was a heavily traveled stretch of highway. However, we saw some interesting homes and landscaping along the way. Arriving at the intersection, there was a lovely little restaurant called Top of the Hill, aptly named, and we called Jim and entered the restaurant and had a nice cold drink while we waited for him. When we first contacted him, he was still on the golf course, but he soon arrived, had a coffee and we were off, back to Fergus, for a nice bite to eat before going on home. Ironically, we arrived back home at 7:00 p.m., exactly twelve hours after we had begun our day. We dropped Jim off, went on to Bernice's, had our tea and pie, and watched a movie. It was *Five People You Meet in Heaven*. It is an interesting concept. The next day, we realized we had missed the Tony Awards. Oh well! Next week, we wouldn't be able to remember who won what anyway. We had had our own interesting day, and our award was 16.3 km more of the Bruce Trail. Not too bad for a couple of old birds (Jim's words). We had somehow gone from a being a couple of *mature ladies* to a couple of *old birds* . . .

After a good night's sleep and a good breakfast, thanks again to Bernice's lovely B & B, I left at 9:00 a.m. for home. We hoped we would be able to get in one more hike before Mother Nature really warmed up for the summer.

Hike No. 40

September 12, 2006

This is our first hike since June because Mother Nature gave us the hottest summer on record, and therefore, we stayed pretty much in the air-conditioning whenever we could. However, the summer seemed to pass quickly, and we were anxious to get back to our hiking. We managed to get it all together for Tuesday, September 12, but much to our chagrin, rain was in the forecast. Being the stalwart adventurers we were, we pushed on anyway, and lo and behold, when we arrived at our destination, it was overcast but not raining.

We started at Jim's at 7:08 a.m. and arrived at the starting point at 9:45 a.m. after stopping for our usual coffee break at Durham. It was rather cool, so we had sweatshirts, jackets, and rain jackets in the event of any bad weather. Off we went into the woods at Highway 6.

We hadn't gone very far when we arrived at Inglis Falls, located in the Inglis Falls Conservation Area. I There are several falls in and around the Owen Sound area, and Bernice took some pictures.

Inglis Falls Hike 40 2006

Continuing, we climbed down a wooden stairway and through some very rocky areas. We needed to be very careful due to previous excessive rainfall and very slippery walking conditions. It was slow going, but we followed the trail to Grey County Road 5, took a left turn, and continued to Concession 3, a 1.3 km stretch, and then back into the bush again. At this point, we hiked through a hardwood bush and followed the brow of the escarpment, where we could view the city of Owen Sound from several points.

Limestone quarries and kilns were below the trail, and there are trails that go down the escarpment to downtown Owen Sound. We took a brief break and rested for about twenty minutes. Continuing along the escarpment, we came to a steep ladder and stairs that lead down to highways 6 and 21. Our devoted chauffeur was waiting a little way down the road. We were so happy to see him, as the rain has started, and we had been hiking for about an hour in the rain and were pretty wet and bedraggled. We might have continued on, but it was 2:30 p.m. We had been hiking for over four hours, and we decided to call it quits. We had gone 12 km. Not too bad, considering the rain, roots, and rocks.

We both had some misgivings about our first hike since June, but we were amazed at how well we felt. Jim had managed to get in a nine-hole golf game while waiting for us but was not happy with his score. The clubs were up for sale again! This was his last chance to attain his goals while we hiked, because we had decided to go at it alone from now on. We planned to take one car, stay at a bread and breakfast (some B & B's cater to hikers) and use it as a base for a three-day hiking session. This way we hoped to make it to Wiarton before the year was done. It was a distance of approximately 65 km. What were we thinking? Jim was really going to miss this adventure, but what could we say? He will be with us when we achieve our goal and reach Tobermory. Ric started us off at Queenston Heights in Niagara, so it is only fitting that Jim joins us at our ending in Tobermory.

We seemed to quickly arrive at Elora for our dinner. We enjoyed the dinner and the rest and then left for home. We actually arrived a little earlier than other times. It was just around 6:00 p.m. We bid farewell to Jim at his place and headed to Bernice's for shower and Jacuzzi time.

Next morning, we plotted our next trip, and I left for home feeling very good about another stretch that we had completed on our way to Tobermory.

Hike No. 41

September 30, 2006

We hoped to continue, if the weather permitted, one more session, staying at a bed and breakfast and hiking for three days. We felt we could accomplish so much more.

This was a five-day effort for me but three for Bernice. I arrived at Bernice's on Friday, September 29, conveniently at suppertime; and she offered up a lovely fare as she always does. She also provided a movie for us to see. *Eight Below* is one of those pictures that didn't get much media attention but offered a wonderful evening's entertainment. We both recommended it as a four-star movie. Having enjoyed dessert with the movie, we went off to bed in good time, as we again were rising early for a long day on Saturday. *Rain* was a major factor, as it was predicted for the entire three days. However, we made up our minds that it was not going to stop us this time. We hoped that the weather predictions would be wrong and Mother Nature would shine on us!

Well, we were right to take the chance as it turned out. It rained steadily as we departed at 7:08 a.m. Saturday morning, September 30, and it rained off and on all the way up. I drove for the first half. We stopped at Harriston, where we had coffee, and Bernice took over, and we arrived at our destination Springmount at 10:10 a.m. There was an information station there and good parking, so we locked the car and headed immediately into the woods over rocks and roots (very familiar ground) and then onto West Street and turned right into Brookholm Conservation Area.

From here, we followed the escarpment edge over deep crevices, where we had to be particularly careful.

Deep Crevasse Hike #41 2006

A lovely view to our right showed a flowerpot formation, and by this time the rain had stopped. We continued along and then descended the escarpment to 19th Street and Park Street, where we stopped at a church and rested, ate an apple, and took shelter, as the rain had started again. It was now 11:45 a.m., and after about a fifteen-minute break, we turned left on to Sommers Street and hiked about 2 km past lovely homes and critiqued them as we passed. We turned onto Range Road and followed along this rural Owen Sound road and then across country until we arrived at a little place called Benallen, on the Gordon Sutherland Parkway. What a surprise that was! It is a little dirt road that intersects with Highway 17. To us city people, this did not describe a parkway! Niagara has a parkway. Prejudiced? I may be! We stopped here for our lunch at about 1:30 p.m. Luckily, it had stopped raining. After our lunch break, we started up Gordon Sutherland Parkway for 1.3 km and then descended the escarpment and wound our way 'round the edge of the escarpment and up some steps to Indian Acres Road.

At this point, Bernice called our hostess, Sue Ann, at the Bramblewood Bed and Breakfast to advise her that we were finished with our hiking. Bernice had made arrangements with Sue Ann that we would stay at her B & B and that she would pick us up when we had finished hiking for the day. Sue Ann soon came along, and after introductions, she drove us back to our car, and then we followed her back to the B & B. It was around 4:00 p.m. While we unloaded some of our stuff, Sue Ann made us a welcome cup of tea, and we visited, got acquainted as she showed us around, and were surprisingly not too tired at all. The excitement of the trip, we assumed.

We freshened up and changed clothes and, at about 6:00 p.m., drove to the Grey County Golf and Country Club, where we had a lovely dinner. This was on the road to Owen Sound, only about fifteen minutes from the B & B. We thoroughly enjoyed a relaxing dinner and found out our server was a young man from Australia who was getting his education in Canada. That's a long way from home! We took our leave, went back to the B & B, and tried to watch a little TV; but indeed found out we were tired, so off to bed we went for a wonderful sleep.

Hike No. 42

October 1, 2006

We awoke on this Sunday, October 1, around 7:30 a.m. (sleeping in for us) and were served a scrumptious breakfast in the upstairs sitting and dining room with a beautiful view of Georgian Bay. Bernice had a nice fresh cup of coffee, and I had a pot of tea while we waited for a smoothie (fresh pineapple, orange, etc.), followed by fresh scones, homemade peach jam, and then an omelet with a side of fresh tomato slices and dill pickles. Very, very tasty! Sue Ann sure wanted us to have lots of energy for the day ahead. When we were ready, Sue Ann drove us to our starting point. We were very happy to see the sun and a comfortable, nice day. At 9:30 a.m., we started off along a very rocky edge of the escarpment until we came to the Gordon Sutherland Parkway again. We had to laugh, as this was definitely not like any parkway we city folks have been accustomed to. This was a dirt track that takes you to the Frank Holley Side Trail. We, however, kept to the main trail and, turning left, came to the East Linton Side Trail, which we passed. Following the main trail, we dropped down through very steep, narrow crevices, larger than some we had seen. They were twenty feet deep in some areas and three to five feet wide.

We gradually ascended back to the top of the escarpment to a mature forest. It was warming up, and we removed some of our outer clothing. We stuffed our sweatshirts in our backpacks and stopped for our lunch at a campsite at noon. Somewhere along this part of the trail, we encountered a very large porcupine that waddled off into the underbrush, probably quite disgusted with the intruders. Bernice, at first, thought it was a bear cub. Gladly, it was not! If it had been a bear cub, we imagined mother bear would have been near, and that would have been a very scary proposition for us. We were in the Glen Management Area with cedar, maple, and oak trees and a view of beautiful treetops. We again headed down through yet another crevice to the bottom of the escarpment. We crossed a stream, skirted some fields, and crossed over a stile that took us to Lindenwood Road. It was 3:30 p.m., and after our call to Sue Ann, she arrived shortly to pick us up. We returned to the B & B for a lovely cup of tea, another visit with Sue Ann, and a refreshing shower. Sue Ann had actually taken us on a little detour to where her husband was finishing up a beautiful flagstone walk for a newly built home in the area. I might mention that their home was a lovely, very-well-planned-out B & B, which they had built three years earlier. A lot of very nice decorating showed the warmth and friendliness that was so apparent in their hospitality. We felt very comfortable and relaxed in the atmosphere provided.

We again went out for dinner but thought we might try one of the restaurants in Owen Sound. However, everything closes down on Sundays in Owen Sound. We finally found a place farther from the downtown district and had a decent meal, but nothing compared with the golf club, which was also closed on Sundays. We had driven around the city for almost an hour, and it 7:00 p.m. before we actually ate, so we were ready to settle down for some relaxation when we arrived back at the B & B. The fresh air and long day made bed seem like a good idea, so we retired, expecting another long day on Monday.

Hike No. 43

October 2, 2006

Monday, October 2, again dawned sunny and quite warm. We were excited to have yet another day of hiking and also looking forward to Sue Ann's great breakfast. Promptly at 8:00 a.m., we were served another delightfully tasty breakfast to assist us on the long day awaiting us. We had a flavorful drink along with muffins, homemade peach jam, French toast, and real maple syrup. I had sausages as well. It was so good!

After finishing our tea and coffee and giving our breakfast a chance to digest, we gathered our things together and followed as Sue Ann led us to our destination. We parked our car on Cole's Road and Concession 20, and then she drove us back to where we would begin and where we had finished the day before. On the way, we saw a flock of sandhill cranes, about fifteen to twenty of them, which Sue Ann said was very unusual. Neither of us had ever seen these birds before, and we were impressed by their size. The wing span looked to be about four feet across. They were in a field quite a ways from us, so it was hard to judge. Sue Ann thought the large number was because they were getting ready to start their migration.

We said good-bye to Sue Ann and thanked her for her hospitality and warm reception and began our day's hike at around 9:45 a.m. on Lindenwood Road. Before long, we encountered another large porcupine that also just waddled away. He was not too interested in us. We progressed along the top of the escarpment, coming very close to the edge at some areas, which necessitated every precaution. It was a heavily wooded area, and as the day warmed up, we again pared down our outer garb. There were many wide crevices here as well. As we hiked along, we believed we had scared up a pheasant. We didn't see it, but it sounded like one, and it was interesting to us that there was so much wildlife on this three-day hike. We decided it was because we were getting farther and farther north and away from the hectic urban life. We had not seen this much wildlife on all our previous hikes.

Three kilometers farther on, we turned north for eight hundred meters and then along an old logging road. At this point we happened to see a large puffball (similar to a huge mushroom) and, looking around, noticed many more of them. This must have been ideal puffball growing conditions. I decided to take a really large one home for Ric.

Ric with puffball.

My dad used to bring home puffballs when he was out hunting. I remembered how they were delicious sautéed in butter. We got out the garbage bags Bernice had brought along, which we would sit on or cower under in case of some serious rain. We put the puffball into the double-bagged bags and tied it to the back of my backpack. Did I resemble the Hunchback of Notre Dame? I could then have both hands free, as the trail again came to an area of wide crevices and rock areas. We were back to the top of the escarpment, and after a few more minutes, we descended down to a large field. At this point, we stopped for a rest and had our energy bars for lunch. I sure was hoping we were getting close to our destination, as my large puffball seemed to be gaining weight.

We estimated it weighted about ten pounds and was getting heavier with each kilometer.

The weather was beautiful, and we had made so much progress in the past two days. We were very pleased with ourselves and willing to keep going to the end. As we walked from the field down to Lundy Lane, we came out to Grey Road or Concession 20 and followed this road to where our car was waiting. I was amazed at the irony of being parked on Cole's Road and hiking down Lundy Lane.

Back home, we lived about six blocks from a main artery named Lundy's Lane in Niagara Falls, and my son's name was Cole. It somehow made me think of home. We were tired but happy and got out of our boots, put all of our stuff in the car, secured the very heavy puffball, and gave Sue Ann a quick call to let her know we had arrived safely back to our car and had successfully finished our hike. We had completed almost 30 km during our stay on this trip.

She, on the other hand, had had a bad day. On her way to town, her car was broadsided by another car. Both cars were severely damaged. It was the other car's fault, however. Sue Ann was shaken, but fortunately there was no serious injury, only some black-and-blue marks and a stiff neck. We offered our sad feelings for her mishap and hoped there would be no further problems. We left for home around 1:30 p.m., having made very good time for the day. I drove as far as Harriston down Highway 3 (which Sue Ann had alerted us to), and it was a lovely route to follow.

There was quite a bit of fall color to the trees, and the terrain was long rolling hills. As we came over one hill, a Mennonite farmer was calmly walking down the highway with five Percheron horses on a rein with five leads. They took up half of the highway and must have been used to traveling that route because they didn't mind us passing by at all. We drove to Harriston and stopped for coffee at Tim Horton's, and Bernice took over the driving. All in all, the trip was really nice, and we had thoroughly enjoyed the weekend. We arrived home around at 4:30 p.m. or 5:00 p.m., had a nice shower and got into our comfies, had a light supper, and relaxed and watched some TV.

I called Ric to tell him we were back, and Jim called to see if we had arrived all in one piece. We were hoping for one more hike in November if Mother Nature will allow it. If not, we had had a wonderful ending to a good year of hiking. We are about 25 km from Wiarton, and if our luck holds, we may be able to complete the trail next year.

Hike No. 44

November 9, 2006

Well, here we are again. Our kind chauffeur offered to drive us one more time to do another's day hike. As the weather in the fall had been mild and we were anxious to do as much as we could, we decided to take him up on his offer and hike one more time in 2006.

November 9, being a Thursday, necessitated that I leave Niagara on Wednesday, which I did. I arrived at Bernice's at dinnertime and brought along Ric's homemade meatballs and sauce, which were very good, as usual. We visited with Jim, but he hurried out the door when he realized we intended to watch the final episode of *Dancing with the Stars*. To our surprise, Emmett Smith won (for those who don't know, he is a football star). I guess being great on the football field helps you become great on the dance floor. He was good anyway, and of course he had the hometown football fans all voting for him.

We were up and away to Jim's in good time. It was an uneventful trip up and, as always a pleasant drive as the roads were fairly quiet. We listened to some good music, and before we knew it, we were at our destination.

Jim dropped us off at Cole's Road and Concession 20. Cole's Road, heading up the escarpment, was a muddy wet mess. The whole center of the road was filled with three or four inches of water. As we edged along the road, a jeep with three young men, dressed for hunting gear, pulled up and stopped and asked us if we were heading up the road. We told them we were. They told us there were other hunters out and about.

They advised us that it was hunting season, and we should be careful. Who knew! Hunting season? We were just hunting for the trail! They seemed rather skeptical of our endeavor. Actually, I think they meant, "Turn around and run from the hills!" However, undaunted, we pushed forth through, muck, guck, and weeds, to the top of the hill where we discovered the other hunters. Incidentally, one chap advised us to make ourselves known in the bush, and I said I had my Girl Guide whistle from a *few* years back and he said, "BLOW IT!" This was not to warn the poor deer but the hunters. However, with no deer, no hunters! We stopped and talked to the six hunters who were taking a break and then moved on, and we believed they thought maybe we were crazy. Not crazy just determined.

We continued on through some wet patches, and then the road became paved and was much easier to hike on. We continued on Cole's Road, a lovely country road, and came to a corner and sat down to eat our lunch. We could see some white cliffs in the distance and decided that was where we were headed.

As we relaxed and enjoyed our lunch, along came a hunter (in full hunting gear) driving an ATV with his gun mounted on the front. He rounded the corner and headed right up the road where we were intending to hike. We soon heard some gunshots and assumed he had spied some poor deer and was out to have him for dinner sometime soon. Before we finished our lunch, he came back down the road and disappeared. This calmed our anxiety a bit. However, as we started out, we heard more gunshots, so I began blowing my whistle as loud as I could. In case we may be mistaken for deer, we opted to stay on the road, which was called Colpoy's Range Road (kind of makes you think of cowboys out on the range).

We followed this road, which was narrow, rutted, and wet. It was slow going, as we had to walk along the edge through tall wet grass and low-hanging bushes. We could hear gunshots now and again, so I continued to blow my whistle. About 2 km down the road, a truck came along with two hunters in it. They passed quite close to us, and if looks could have killed, we would never have finished our hike. Our assumption was that we had probably scared all the deer away with my whistle blowing, and the hunters were not pleased to see what had frightened their quarry. Two more hunters passed shortly thereafter and viewed us with equal disdain. We guessed these hunters did not consider this day a good hunt.

Just as we turned to head up the escarpment to meet Jim, another truck came along with one man in it. Although he didn't identify himself, we believe he may have been a game warden checking out the hunters. Or maybe the hunters had called him and informed him of the "intruders." He stopped and asked us where we were headed. When we told him, he informed us there was no road into the bush where we were to meet Jim. Again we had somehow (surprisingly) misinterpreted the map, so the warden gave us directions for a small detour. We called Jim, and thankfully he was able to meet us on Centre Road. We shook our heads in amazement. How did we do it? This was approximately 11.9 km, and we were closing in on Wiarton, and with our dogged determination, we would be there next year.

Jim steered us on home, and we stopped at our favorite restaurant in Elmira, had a very nice dinner, and were back to Cambridge around 7:00 p.m. and soon back to Bernice's. Bed sure looked inviting, and we were soon taking advantage of the comfort it afforded.

I headed home early the next morning, and we planned for a get-together with Mary before Christmas, if the weather held. Although the distance is relatively short, the weather can be very bad down Niagara way and just fine in the Cambridge area. Conversely, it can also be the other way around. So the weather is always a consideration.

We had accomplished quite a lot in 2006 and were very pleased. We were, however, anxiously looking forward to the spring of 2007 to try and wind up the whole trail. We will probably do a three-day trip, or maybe more, to accomplish more with each trip up. It is really the best way to "git 'er dun." At any rate, we are hoping for a healthy new year to continue our feat. Thanks to Jim for driving us so many times and urging us on and listening to our tales of woe at the end of the day.

So here's to 2007 and Tobermory!
MAP #3 Owen Sound to Tobermory
June 19 2009

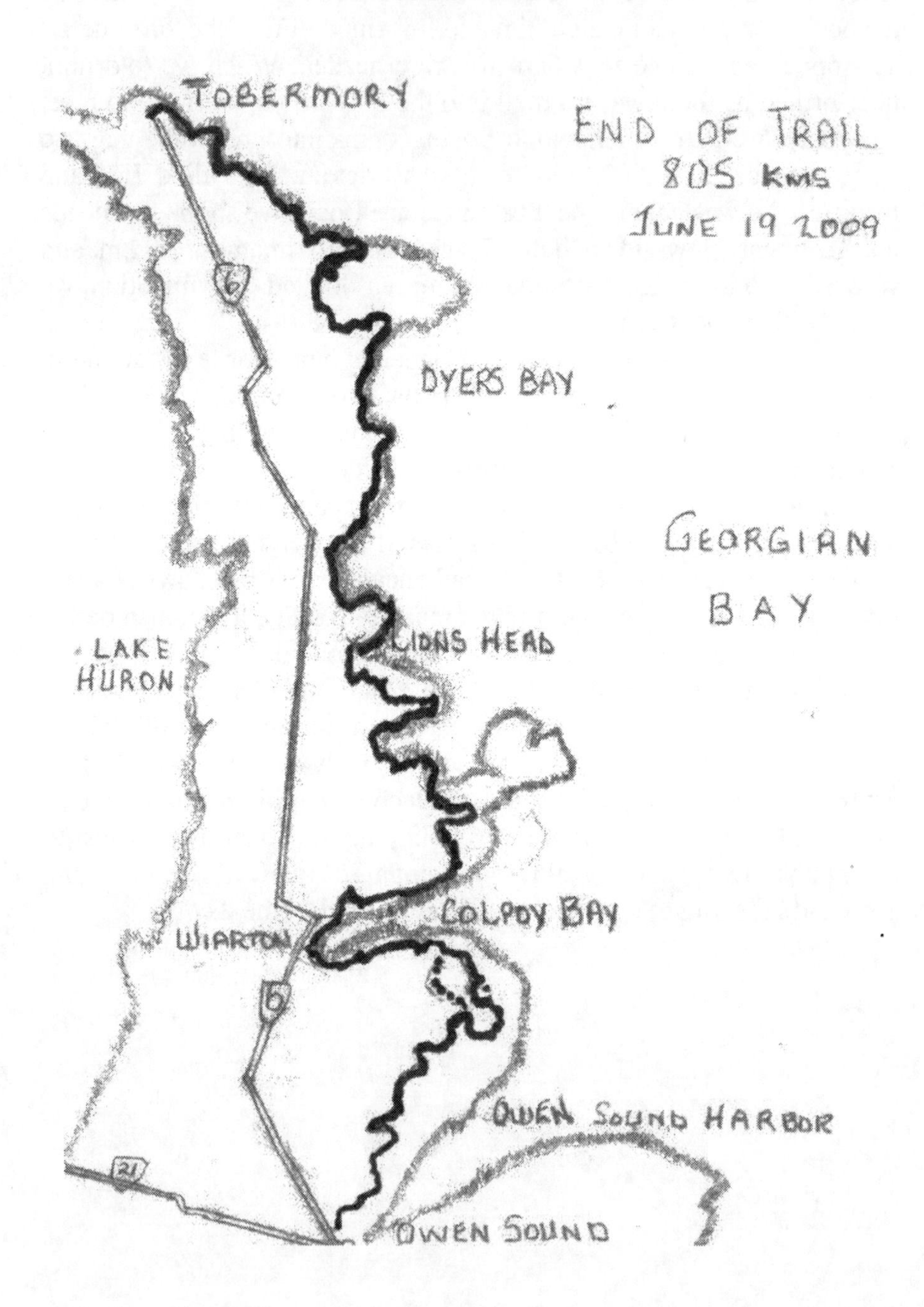

Hike No. 45

June 6, 2008

It was now June of 2008. It had taken some time to get back to our hiking because in January of 2007 my husband, Ric, began radiation and chemotherapy for cancer he had been diagnosed with late in December 2006. After long and arduous months of treatment, Ultra sounds, CAT scans surgery, and more treatments, he was well on the road to recovery. It had been a tough year for Ric, but he carried on admirably, and he was feeling so much better, almost back to normal. We felt we could now continue with our odyssey. We had chosen this weekend to begin, and did we pick a winner! We had decided to stay at a Bed and Breakfast for three days rather than drive back and forth so often. We accomplished all we set out to do in our three-day outing, but we really paid for it in sweat. No blood or tears but plenty of sweat.

To begin, I had arrived at Bernice's Thursday, June 5, at dinnertime (of course). I took a different route up the Queen Elizabeth Way to the Red Hill Valley Parkway to Copetown and up to Highway 8 and Cambridge. It was a quicker route than some of the others I had taken. I was met with a pleasant surprise, as Mary was there to join us for dinner. I hadn't seen Mary or Bernice for some time, and it was a pleasure for me to be among old friends again. Bernice always came up with a delicious menu, and we enjoyed dinner and getting caught up with events. Mary filled us in on a reunion she had attended with some schoolmates. We had some laughs and reminisced about school days. I recalled my visit to see my daughter in Iqualuit in Nunavut, which is north of the 60th

Parallel. It was farther north than I had ever been and certainly different. Barren and ice covered land and very cold temperatures, such as minus 40°F in May, are the usual weather conditions. Nice place to visit but wouldn't want to live there. After a pleasant evening, we managed to get to bed by 11:00 p.m. to be ready for an early rise.

We awoke at 5:30 a.m. on Friday, June 6, eager to get started. After a tasty breakfast and a check in with the weather channel, we loaded up the car and started out at about 7:00 a.m. We began the drive with renewed excitement because we were again getting back to our "wanderings and adventures." It was hot, and the temperature continued to climb. Thank goodness for air-conditioning. We had a really nice drive and arrived at our starting place, which was at Gleason Lake Road and Colpoy's Range Road.

We left there and hiked to Bruce Caves and on to Spirit Rock Side Trail, We crossed a logging road into a bush leading to Grey Road 26 and on through a little place called Oxeden. Continuing, we climbed over a stile onto a road leading to Wiarton Airport. We skirted the edge of the airport, which was quite small. When we came to a little stream, as the heat was increasing, I filled one of my water bottles with water from the stream. It seemed as though a nice cold mini shower would be nice when we get to the boiling point, which seemed to be coming on quickly.

We crossed the stream and through a field and came to yet another stile. We had gone a considerable distance in the blazing sun, so we took advantage of the stile to sit down and rest. Bernice was especially feeling the effects of the heat and, as she sat down, said she could just go to sleep. I believed she was suffering from heat exhaustion and insisted she drink some water, and I soaked my knitted water-bottle holder with water and placed it on the back of her neck. She splashed some water on her face and began to feel somewhat better. I was afraid she was going to pass out, but the water did the trick, and in a few minutes, we continued on. We hiked a short distance and descended a ladder and some steps and came out on Mary Street in Wiarton. We had completed 12.7 km. We rested near a large building and called Sue Ann for a ride back to the B & B. We felt exhausted, but after a nice shower and a cool drink and a few minutes to relax, we left for Owen Sound for a lovely dinner at the Rocky Raccoon. We enjoyed our dinner and had a visit from the chef, who was interested in our hiking trek. We then headed back to the B & B and a very early bed.

Hike No. 46

June 7, 2008

We started our day on Saturday at Bluewater Park on the waterfront in Wiarton. Of course, we saw Wiarton Willie, who is commemorated by a lovely carved image of himself in the park. Willie is Canada's answer to USA's Punxsutawney Phil. Both of these groundhogs come out in the spring to inform us whether we will have more winter weather or an early spring.

MAP 3

We hiked past Spirit Rock, which tells the story of the Indian maid who, from this rock, jumped to her death to join her departed lover.

Legend of Spirit Rock Hike 46 2008

We continued into the bush, and at one point, we climbed an iron spiral staircase taking us up the escarpment with a lovely view of the bay. We carried on to the Crawford Road side trail and, at this point, called Sue Ann to pick us up. We walked along the Mallory Beach area along Colpoy's Bay, and soon Sue Ann came along the road and met up with us. We had completed 12.8 km. This had been a fairly easy hike, and the weather had been ideal. We drove back to the B & B, and we relaxed with Sue Ann and her husband, Wayne, on the porch. We talked about the beautiful view from there of the bay and the beauty of the area in general. Feeling somewhat refreshed, we then went out again for dinner and returned back to the B & B to reflect on the day's hike and go over our maps for the next day's hike.

Hike No. 47

June 8, 2008

On Sunday, June 8, we started at Crawford Road on a beautiful sunny day with a light breeze blowing. We stopped to view Georgian Bay and a campsite on the shore. The view of the bay was wonderful, and the light breeze created different colors in the water.

View of Georgian Bay Hike 47, 2008

We continued along the escarpment edge and then continued westward over a grassland, over a stile, and into a pasture. We finished at Coveney's Side Trail and had completed 8.3 km for a total of 33.8 km in three days. We arrived at our car and were ready for the drive home. It was a great finish to our three days of hiking.

Driving home, we missed a turn (what else is new?). This led to more of our wanderings. However, we ended up enjoying a Sunday drive around the area. We eventually found our way to the main highway and ended up at Bernice's home in the early evening. We had some leftovers at Bernice's for our supper and had a very early bedtime.

After breakfast, I left for home. It had been quite a weekend. However, we had a feeling of accomplishment. We will make some new plans in the near future.

Hike No. 48

August 20, 2008

We've moved on to Wednesday, August 20, 2008, and I arrived at Bernice's on the night before beginning our hike. We perused the maps, as it is becoming more difficult to balance the kilometers we can hike in a day with the drop-off and pickup points available now that we are in the more northerly, less populated area. Having finalized our plans, we were off for a good night's rest. We were staying again at Sue Ann's but would begin our hike first and then call for a ride back to our car.

Having packed the car the night before, we left at 6:40 a.m., Wednesday morning, a little earlier than we usually managed to get away. It was a beautiful morning, just the kind you want for a good hiking day. We arrived at Coveney's Side Road at about 10:30 a.m. and prepared for the day. Heading north up the road, we arrived at Knapp's Lookout and soon turned into the woods. In a large maple woodlot, we saw something on the trail, which turned out to be a survey monument with the name of the surveyor, Ivan Dinsmore. There was a plaque on the monument stating that a very large fine was to be paid if it was tampered with. We wondered if this commemorated early surveying of the surrounding territory. It was an interesting find.

We met two couples from Toronto heading back the way we had just come. We were headed to the Cape Croker Indian Reserve, and as we descended the hill toward the reserve, we again met up with the same couples. They advised us that we couldn't go through the reserve to the side road farther along the way, where we had arranged to meet Sue Ann as the road was closed. So we called her and arranged to meet her back at the entrance to the reserve.

While we waited, we decided to go into the little snack bar just outside the reserve. We hadn't seen anything quite like that in a long while. They had everything for hunting, fishing, etc., but nothing seemed to be in order. You had to serve yourself tea or coffee. We did manage to get a hamburger, and it was very good. Sue Ann arrived at about 3:00 p.m., and we were glad to get back to our car and arrived at Sue Ann's B & B. We had a cool drink and a good visit with Sue Ann. We decided to go to Wendy's for a quick supper. We got back to the B & B around 8:00 p.m., and bed soon beckoned. It had been quite a long drive and, plus the hike, we were ready for a good rest.

Hike No. 49

August 21, 2008

Next morning, we were up early at 8:30 a.m., Thursday, August 21, for our hike no. 49 and were anxious to get started, as we were farther and farther from our starting point. We started at the reservation and the Jones Bluff Side Trail and crossed over a side road and entered the bush again. We followed the Snake Trail, a boardwalk built by the Indians with wood supplied by five Bruce Trail clubs. We followed Camp Road to the foot of the escarpment, where it rises steeply on a steel staircase (twenty-four steps) to the top of the escarpment again. There is a lovely view of Sydney Bay. We continued along the top with occasional views of the bay. A ladder led down to the base, across a small stream, and came out on Cottage Road. Cottages lined the road along the beach that led to Hope Bay.

We had stopped for a bit of lunch, and who should we meet up with again but the folks from Toronto who were on their way home. We walked on down the road to a general store and waited for Sue Ann. The sandy beach of Hope Bay and the blue water of the bay enticed us to take off our boots and stand in the water for a few minutes. It was a real treat for the feet after a 10.2 km hike.

After a seemingly long ride back to the B & B, we did our usual shower, cool drink, and relaxation routine. Sue Ann asked us to help her plan a new iris bed she was intending to plant. Wayne had worked hard on the preparation of the bed, together with a nice stone walkway back to the garden shed. We did our best and then left for a lovely dinner at the golf and country club. Sue Ann had planted her iris garden by the time we returned, and we hoped to have a chance to see it in bloom. After a long day and the anticipation of another long day to follow, we headed off to bed early.

Hike No. 50

August 22, 2008

Friday, August 22, dawned warm and humid, so we hurriedly had another of Sue Ann's wonderful breakfasts, and Sue Ann drove, and we followed to the beginning point of our day. Initially, the trail was not too difficult, but we were on an ascent-descent program at which time we saw the glacier potholes. The holes had been created by the glaciers and were as round as a bowl, and one was about four feet across and ten to twelve feet deep, it appeared, although it was difficult to tell because the bottom was covered with leaves.

Glacier Pot Holes Hike 50 2008

Here at the top of the escarpment again was a beautiful view of the bay. It was getting very warm, and the humidity was building. As we continued along, partway below the top of the escarpment, we encountered a complete rocky section with big boulders and shale in large amounts. The rocks were moss covered, and one had to be very careful of the footing. We maneuvered the rocks and shale for 1.5 km, but it felt like 15 km. It was very slow going due to the heat and humidity, and we became exhausted, necessitating frequent stops and drinks to try to cool off. We were very surprised when we suddenly came to the road where our car was parked across the road. With the water we had left, we had mini showers, changed into dry clothes, and drove back to Sue Ann's. We had made it! It had been a tough one, what with the trail itself and the heat and humidity.

We had decided to stay at another bed and breakfast farther north and closer to Lion's Head so that on our next trip, we could be closer to that area. We were reluctant to move on though, as Sue Ann and Wayne had not only been perfect hosts but had also become friends, and we would miss them. We promised to keep in touch and to stop in, and we will be sure to have them join us for a celebration when we reach the Northern Terminus at Tobermory. We said our good-byes, thanked Sue Ann for all her help and encouragement, and headed for home.

We had been hiking from 9:45 a.m. until 3:45 p.m. It had been a long hard day, and we were glad to be going home. We stopped on the way for coffee, and Bernice drove the rest of the way. I was totally exhausted.

Jim was waiting at Bernice's with hamburgers and corn on the cob for our supper when we finally arrived home at 7:00 p.m. We brought Jim up to date on our ordeal, and he left early so we could collapse in bed. I arose early, and after thanking Bernice once again for her hospitality, I left for home and arrived at 10:30 a.m. We would have to wait for cooler weather to continue, perhaps late September or early October. We didn't want to hit the hunting season again. We had completed 31 km.

Hike No. 51

September 26, 2008

We were on our last hike for 2008 at Hope Bay Area. September had arrived, and checking weather reports for September 25 and the following few days, it appeared we were looking good. So on Thursday, I arrived at Bernice's in time for another free meal. We headed off to bed early, as we had a long day ahead.

We packed up early in the morning on Friday, the twenty-sixth, for a long drive of almost four hours. We made our usual stop along the way and got a good stretch and coffee before we continued on, arriving at our destination at 10:30 a.m. We parked our car and followed a cart track, which climbed the escarpment with some beautiful sights of Hope Bay. We followed a bush road among huge boulders into a forest and the top of the Georgian Bay shoreline. We turned left and crossed the Alvar, an area of limestone with little or no topsoil. There was minimal vegetation. This was a very routine hike, and we continued on until we came to the intersection of Scenic Caves Road and Rush Cove Road.

We awaited our new bed-and-breakfast hostess, Jennifer, of the 45th Parallel B & B in Lion's Head. We introduced ourselves, and we drove back to pick up our car. It was now 4:00 p.m. We were happy to unpack our things, shower, and get to know our new home and hostess for the coming couple of days. We went out for a nice dinner at the Lion's Head Inn and soon returned for an early bed. It had been a long drive and a long hike, but we had happily completed 12 km, and tomorrow was another day.

Hike No. 52

September 27, 2008

We had planned to have Sue Ann from our previous B & B join us on this Saturday hike. After a 7:30 a.m. breakfast call, which Jennifer prepared for us and which we enjoyed, we gathered our gear, and Jennifer drove us to McCague Road at Barrow Bay where we were meeting Sue Ann. Sue Ann arrived, and we had a little visit with her. A man and his Great Dane, very large but also very friendly, was out for his morning jaunt. We chatted with the man and admired his dog and soon decided we had better begin.

Off we went down the road, and after a few minutes (stopping to look around and stop our chatting), we realized we were headed the wrong way. Who else but us could be so confused? Too much talking, too little walking. Amid red faces and some laughs, we returned to the beginning and started again. We followed McCague Road, which eventually takes you right into Lion's Head Provincial Park. We took the Inland Side Trail after about 2 km, and we followed a yellow-blazed trail and came upon a geodetic benchmark. This is located exactly on the 45th Parallel halfway between the North Pole and the equator. It seemed strange to be standing in that place.

We soon joined the McCague Road again and followed right along the edge of the escarpment. This provides some spectacular lookouts for Cape Chin, White Bluff, and Isthmus Bay. While taking in the views of these lookouts, at times we were perched on the edges of some huge rock cliffs of the escarpment very high above the water. At one point, along came a group of students with huge backpacks. They were hiking and camping for the weekend on the trail heading southward. We also met a young couple with their baby in a backpack. That seemed like a good way to the hike the trail. We arrived at a dirt road and came out of the bush on Moore Street and Lion's Head Beach Park and downtown Lion's Head.

Bernice & Sue Ann Hike 52 2008

We sat down opposite the local hospital on a stone wall on Moore Street and contemplated entering the hospital for a complete rest. It had been a long exhausting day, but we pushed on up the long hill from downtown Lion's Head to Jennifer's Bed and Breakfast. It seemed much longer than it really was. We finally arrived at the B & B thoroughly tired from a long but very interesting hike and day. We drove Sue Ann to her car and assured her we would be in touch. We returned to rest before we went out for dinner.

We were thoroughly done in this trip. It had been an extremely hot day, and ending up walking up that long hill in Lion's Head really finished us off. After a soothing bath, a refreshing cool drink, and a good rest, we drove to a little restaurant in Ferndale for our dinner. There was a small gift shop next to the restaurant, and we still had energy enough to look around at the items they had to offer. As we entered the restaurant, we saw the same couple with the baby that we had seen on the hike, also at dinner there. We were happy to see they too had managed to finish the hike in good shape. We had a nice dinner and returned shortly to the B & B eager to immerse ourselves in the comfort of our beds.

Hike No. 53

September 28, 2008

Thursday morning saw us up and away early after a nice breakfast, which Jennifer again prepared for us. We packed up our things, and Jennifer led the way to Rush Cove Road, the end point of our hike. We left our car there, and she returned us to Lion's Head and the beginning of our last day on this stretch of the Bruce.

The trail actually took us along Highway 9, and then we turned left onto Scenic Caves Road. We were hiking back along Whipporwill Bay. I had begun to feel twinges in my lower right back, a two-minute stop every once in a while seemed helpful. Guess I am joining the rest of my age group and beginning to feel the signs of aging. I assure you I don't like it. However, climbing up and over and down on the rocks didn't bother me a bit. I guess I will have to stick to the hills. We arrived back at our car and started the next lap, our ride back to civilization and the hectic rush of urban life.

Jim was awaiting our arrival back at Bernice's with a very inviting barbecue dinner. After visiting for a while, we turned in early. It had been another long day. The next morning, I left around 9:00 a.m. for home. This was the last of our hikes for 2008. We always feel nostalgic about finishing up for the year and hope the spring will see us out and hiking again.

With any luck, we will make it to Tobermory next year and reach the end of our wanderings and adventures.

Hike No. 54

May 26, 2009

Here we go again! This was to be the first hike of 2009. On May 27, Wednesday, we began our hike with anticipation and some trepidation as to our stamina after nine months of inaction. It seemed kind of like a pregnancy—eager for the day, but with a definite desire to get the whole thing over with. We would be staying again at Jennifer's 45th Parallel B & B.

I had arrived on Tuesday, the twenty-sixth, at Bernice's, had dinner; and we spent quite some time reviewing our last hike. Due to faulty human and technical errors, our hike did not get transcribed. We did, however, get up to date after much map reading and brainstorming and were ready to start early in the morning. It was somewhat overcast, but as the day progressed, the sun came out, and it was a perfect day for hiking. We had a coffee break at Hanover and continued on to our destination at Cape Chin South Road. We were in the municipality of Northern Bruce Peninsula. With still about 60-65 km to go, we, nevertheless, felt like we were going to conquer the Bruce after all. Just not that day!

We parked our car and started into the bush, hiking along a fairly easy and well-marked route. The trail skirted a large body of water, and we saw beaver dams and walked over wooden walkways through marshy wetlands. Around 12:45 p.m., we stopped for lunch and sat on some nice, wide, flat rocks. When we had finished, we packed up for the last lap of the hike. Just then, we saw the most adorable little green-and-yellow-striped snake sunning himself not more than three feet from my hand. Yessss! *Eeeek!* broke the quiet of the woods, and I shuddered to think I had been sitting next to him, quietly enjoying my lunch. Snakes are my least favorite members of wildlife. However, as he had not disturbed us—well, at least not intentionally—we did not disturb him and hurried on down the path, jingling our bells to warn the bears of their impending doom should they show themselves to us. (Or maybe it was our impending doom?) If there were any bears in the area though, they decided not to show themselves, for which we were very thankful.

Shortly, we arrived at a stile, which Bernice smartly stepped over and I not so smartly ducked underneath and caught my backpack on the wire. Reaching to undo this dilemma, I got a slight shock, which I fortunately survived, enabling us to continue our hike. Apparently, the fence was charged to keep the large herd of Black Angus within the pasture. We crossed over an adjoining field, over another stile, and entered another wooded area, arriving at Cape Chin North Road. After another fifteen minutes or so, we arrived at the accommodations we were proposing to stay in on our next hike, namely Cape Chin Connection Country Inn. We had a nice lunch and a lovely cup of tea and were shown around by Velma of the inn. We decided we would continue from this bed and breakfast on our, possibly, last hike.

We continued another fifteen minutes up the road to Borchardts Road where Jennifer from the 45th Parallel B & B picked us up and drove us to our car. We followed her back to the B & B. We had our dinner at Mom's Restaurant in Ferndale, came home, talked for a few minutes with Jennifer, and turned in early so we would be rested for yet another day on the trail.

Hike No. 55

May 27, 2009

We arose this Wednesday morning, May 27, 2009, to a heavy mist, making it hard to see anything. We decided to hike anyway and hope the mist would lift as the morning passed. We had a nice breakfast, and at 8:30 a.m., Willy, Jennifer's husband, kindly drove ahead of us to our finishing point for the day and, after parking our car, drove us to the beginning of our hike at Forty Road and the Richardson Side Trail.

Getting our gear altogether, we headed into the bush, over rocky terrain, where we shortly joined the Bruce Trail.

On The Trail Hike 55 2009

Apparently, there are some wonderful views from this part of the trail. However, visibility was *zero*. We hiked along the top of the escarpment, passing White Bluffs Side Trail, Dogwood Side Trail, and also Whippoorwill Side Trail, to the cutoff at Reed's Dump. Prior to Reed's Dump area, we had met up with some hikers who were from Dundas, Ontario, and St. George, Ontario. These places are nearby Cambridge, so we felt like we had met folks from home. They were doing the same stretch but hiking from north to south. There were about ten of them, and they too were seniors wondering what we were all doing out in the wilderness on such a dismal rainy day. I'm sure they were of the same opinion as we—that when the hike is completed, a profound feeling of accomplishment overcomes you, and believe it or not, it all seems worth it.

We continued on the Cape Chin Side Trail for 1.5 km, and just prior to that, we had seen some fresh bear scat right on the trail. We somehow didn't seem too anxious. I guess due to the cold and wet, we simply couldn't muster up any fear. A little excitement may have raised the body temperature, naturally warming us and making us a more interesting meal for the bear. But it didn't happen, so we continued on and, very soon, saw through the trees a great sight. Our car was waiting on the side road. We removed our wet clothes, donned comfy dry ones, and drove back to the welcoming B & B. We relaxed with a hot toddy to warm the cockles of our hearts and recalled the adventures of the day. We again had our dinner at the Lion's Head Inn. Too much food was served, but we ate what we could, and it was tasty fare. Back at the B & B, we caught up with news on the TV and then were off to bed.

Hike No. 56

May 28, 2009

The next morning, Thursday, May 28, after being dropped off, we began at Forty Road and hiked along Whippoorwill Bay, leading us back into Lion's Head. It was again overcast and foggy, but we had only a 4.9 km hike for the day. We had an uneventful foray, and we arrived back at the B & B at 9:45 a.m. After packing up the car, we bade farewell to Jennifer, thanked her for her hospitality, and headed home.

The drive home was uneventful. We stopped at Harriston, at the Cedar Rail, for a break, a place Bernice and her husband, Dave, had often stopped at on the their trips, back and forth, up north to their cottage. We made excellent time and were home by 2:00 p.m.

Jim had hamburgers ready for us upon our arrival at Bernice's. The hamburgers were great and really filled the bill. As we had made such good time both hiking and traveling, I decided to go on home after our burgers. I bid farewell to Jim and Bernice and hoped to see them in the near future. Bernice and I were really pleased with our trip and were anxiously looking forward to the next and, hopefully, our final trip. It would be a real thrill to finally reach our goal, which we had begun so many years before.

Hike No. 57

June 15, 2009

Well, this would be the beginning of the end. We were heading north for the, hopefully, final lap of our Bruce Trail odyssey. We planned to stay at the Cape Chin Connection Bed and Breakfast for the week of June 15-19 and complete this adventure.

I arrived in late afternoon of the June 14 at Bernice's. We had a very nice dinner, and later, Jim came to wish us well. We turned in fairly early so we would be up and ready for a long day. We arose at 5:30 a.m. and pulled out of Bernice's driveway at 6:30 a.m., excited to be nearing the end of our long trail. We decided to each take our own vehicle so that we could finish at our own pace.

After our usual coffee break in Hanover, we finally arrived in the general area of where we were hiking for the day. However, best-laid plans—you know. It took some fancy maneuvering to finally get one car at the end of the hike and one at the beginning. While we were parking at the beginning of the trail, we met a friendly farmer inquiring as to our purpose. People seem to be curious when they see a couple of ole girls out in the middle of nowhere. It seemed normal to us! We were just doing our thing. Anyway, when he found out our intentions, he informed us of the bear population, which he thought was above average for the year. Also snakes appeared to be in excess. What a treat for us! Bernice would have rather faced a snake, and I was for the bear all the way. Those crawly things just give me the creeps. Hopefully, those creatures of nature will make themselves scarce when we are around. The farmer had a field full of cattle and one big bull in the group. He was calling to them from his truck and driving down the road, a modern day cowboy in his pickup. and they all followed along across the field. I think it was lunchtime. It was an amusing sight.

We finally got started at 12:30 p.m. at Cape Chin Road North and Borchardts Road and headed north, arriving at Devil's Monument about one hour later.

Devil's Monument Hike #57 2009

The rock formation resembles a flowerpot. This is a very interesting natural landmark. There were also some beautiful views from the escarpment high above the bay. Looking back to Cape Chin and forward to Cabot Head were breathtaking views. The terrain was difficult, very rocky, and lots of up, down, and over areas for quite a distance. We came to the Britain Lake Road and chose to continue on up the road until we came to the Laird Side Trail, which again meets the Bruce Trail at Dyers Bay Road.

In this immediate area is Gillies Lake where my husband and I had spent our holidays many years ago. I had never anticipated hiking here many years later.

We were pleased to see a profusion of Jack-in-the-Pulpits and some, we believe, orchids. Also, there were birds cheerily breaking the silence with their lovely songs. Along the Juniper Flats Side Trail, which sounds like something out of an old Western movie, we were fighting off hordes of mosquitoes. Bernice somehow made contact with the rocks, facedown. The rocks fared well. Bernice did not. She suffered a gash over her eye and abrasions on her right shoulder and left knee. Fortunately, it was not as serious as it might have been. After some first aid, we resumed our hike.

We were very tired by this time, which may have contributed to Bernice's fall, and were anxious to finish the hike. We still had probably 1.5 km to go. So we "sucked 'er up" and "got 'er done." We finally reached the car at around 5:30 p.m., a full twelve hours since we started out in the morning. We had completed 8.6 km on the trail. We drove to pick up my car and ended up at Cape Chin Connection at 6:15 p.m. After such a long day, dinner on the patio was a really nice ending. We sat outside for a few minutes, enjoying the warm summer evening. We got our stuff out of the cars and headed for our room for some well-earned relaxation and sleep.

Hike No. 58

June 16, 2009

Day no. 2, Tuesday, June 16, dawned sunny and bright, and after a very enjoyable breakfast, we left looking for a place to park. We finally got Bernice's car parked at the National Park Reserve parking lot, which cost us $11.70 for a day's parking. We thought that was a little pricey but later had a change of mind. We started at 11:15 a.m. and began a very strenuous 7 km hike. As suggested by some information we had obtained, we decided to do the hike from north to south, as the terrain was part of the most difficult of the entire Bruce Trail and seemed easier if done from north to south.

We trekked along over huge boulders, struggling to get up and then struggling to get down again. A young chap came bounding along over the rocks, making it look so easy, while we crawled along with difficulty. We stopped a moment and found out he was from Guelph, Ontario, another city within a twenty-five-mile radius of Cambridge. He was working for RIM (Research in Motion) of Waterloo, Ontario, the company responsible for the Blackberry. We also encountered a group of six people ironically from Bernice's church in Cambridge. We knew they were hiking the Bruce but had no idea we would come upon them in the far reaches of Northern Ontario. They were just starting the more difficult terrain as we were coming to the easier part. Also, along the way were a woman and her mother, who were also hiking the Bruce.

It was beginning to get very warm in the midday, and we chose to take a side trail, hoping to end up at the shore. To reach the shore, there was a rope descent, which, for us at this point, was a little too ambitious. We found a cool spot in some shade and removed our boots and socks, soothed our sore feet, and cooled off with a lovely breeze coming in from the bay.

Refreshed, we began the easier part of the trail—just a nice walk in the park, so to speak. As we walked along the nice wide path through a lovely treed area, with the sun streaking through the trees, we saw a not-too-friendly-looking Massassauga rattlesnake sunning himself right in the middle of the path. We just stopped and waited for him to slither away into the foliage at the side of the path. We also saw some bear scat but, thankfully, no bears. We had heard some stories from our B & B hostess Ann Bard of bears in the vicinity. Apparently, there was one old bear and several young ones. I guess they weren't any more anxious to see us than we were to see them.

We were passed along the way by two runners, who we believed to be part of a group running from Tobermory to Niagara for a charitable organization. I had heard about it on my car radio driving up. They were doing it from Tuesday to Saturday, 894 km. They ran past us as if we were standing still. However, the approximate age difference was forty-some odd years, which may have accounted for the difference in speed.

It was now 5:30 p.m., and we were anxiously looking for the spot where we had parked my car. As we exited the wooded area and reviewed the trail map, we realized our car was another one and a half hours down the road. To say we were tired is an understatement.

However, we did make it and arrived back at the inn at 8:45 p.m., just in time to get a wonderful bowl of Moroccan chicken soup. Did that ever hit the spot! We spent a few minutes in the hot tub, fell into bed, and didn't wake until 8:15 a.m. *What a day it had been!*

Hike No. 59

June 17, 2009

This day you will never believe! We didn't awaken until 8:15 a.m., so we hurriedly got dressed, quickly ate breakfast, drove to Emmett Lake at the National Park Reserve, and left my car there. In Bernice's car, we continued on to Cyprus Lake to leave Bernice's car and start our hike. It was such a busy place. Busloads of high school students, another group of about twelve to fourteen people, a couple with a teenage boy, and two or three more groups were all at various stages of preparation for a day's hike. This was the Cyprus Lake Campground, with several camping areas and a huge parking lot. We started down Horsetail Lake Road, which brought us to the edge of Georgian Bay and a pebble beach, about 0.6 km from the parking area.

Georgian Bay We Went Wrong Way Hike 59 2009

From there we could see the Natural Arch and the Grotto. These dolomite formations were created from years of the waters of Georgian Bay crashing against the shore.

It was a lovely Wednesday, sunny with cloudy intervals, and just right for hiking. We watched all the people heading out for a day of hiking. After crawling over some huge rocks, we reached the cobblestone beach.

Cobblestone Beach Hike 59 2009

According to the Bruce Trail guide, part of the area we were intending to hike was extremely rugged and remote with no access to water for 6 km. The beach was about 1,000 yards long, and then the trail entered into the woods. Shortly, the other people disappeared, and we continued on at our own pace, enjoying the view along the escarpment. We had intended to hike from north to south as recommended due to the challenging and rugged trail. We kept up a pretty good pace, and we eventually came to a hardwood forest with little underbrush. We estimated we had hiked about 5 km. We kept up the pace but didn't seem to arrive at our destination. We got to the shore of Loon Lake, and it was about 5:30 p.m. We emerged from the woods to another cobblestone beach. On the far side was a sign saying it was 8 km to the next available water. We had only completed about 6 or 7 km, but it seemed much farther. We finally realized we had headed north rather than south as we had planned. It was becoming overcast, and a wind was picking up. There was no way we were heading into the woods at that time of the evening, and to go back was not an option either. We sat down on the rocks and contemplated our dilemma. It appeared the only option we had was to call 911. Upon receiving an operator and giving particulars, such as our names, ages, hiking experience, and the food and water available to us, the dispatcher passed my call over to the OPP. They told us to sit tight and wait for a call. The OPP contacted the Nation Park Service and Rescue Unit who, in turn, contacted us. Again, giving all the vital information and more discussion, they decided to come by boat to pick us up. The alternative was for us to remain where we were and they would come by ATV and pick us up in the morning. They didn't think we would fair too well overnight on the open beach. We certainly agreed.

We positioned ourselves as comfortably as possible on a pile of stones and, looking north, waited for the rescue boat, which they said would arrive in fifteen to twenty minutes. We began to feel pretty embarrassed to think of the predicament we had put ourselves in.

National Marine Service Rescue Boat Hike59 June 17 2009

Within fifteen minutes, we could see them crossing the water. It seemed like a long way away, but they arrived very quickly. They asked us to walk over the cobblestones to a deeper area of water so they could bring the boat close to land. It proved rather interesting to see two old birds trying to stretch over huge rocks with about three feet of space between rocks and boat. With their help and encouragement, we "got 'er dun." However, we felt very embarrassed at our folly. They were kind and assured us we had definitely done the right thing, and once aboard, we began our trip back to the National Park Service Marine Unit in Tobermory. The OPP officer Jon Malott was a very friendly chap, and the safety dispatch person from the NPS Rescue Unit was a lovely young woman, named Katherine Welch. The boat's Captain Ernie Wyonch was also helpful and friendly. Assisting was Safety Officer Sesilina Rouault, also friendly and helpful. They joked and kidded with us and relaxed a tense situation and again assured us we had done the right thing.

They inquired as to how long we had been hiking the trail, and we had to tell them it had been almost eight years. Because of our age and the time of day, they had decided they had better bring us in by boat.

During the boat ride back, Bernice decided to divulge the information that her license, ownership, and insurance information was mistakenly left back at home. Our friendly OPP officer made a couple of comments, and Bernice asked what she should do, and he replied, "Just don't get stopped by the OPP." We had a good laugh over that! He then informed us though that the information he had "would cost us." Well, during the ride back to Tobermory, we got up to approximately $200 in $50 increments for one thing and another. It certainly was a laugh all the way. They certainly made us feel less ridiculous. When we landed on the dock, Bernice had them pose for a picture and later sent them a thank-you note and a copy of the picture. We certainly appreciated their humor and kindness in our unfortunate situation.

Welcome Rescue Team Ernie Katharine Jon Sesilina

We were ushered into a large formal room and seated ourselves around a very large conference table for our "debriefing." During this time, a comment was made that they had missed their dinner, so I suggested pizza and wings—another $50 or so. My offer was declined, and again laughter broke out.

After again giving all the details of our unfortunate situation, it was decided that our OPP officer would return us to our car parked back in the park. It was now nearly 8:00 p.m. Officer Jon waited until we started the car and was sure we were okay and then wished us good luck on the rest of the hike. We thanked him for his help, and we both took our leave. He headed back to his dispatch office, and we went to find someplace to eat. We ended up back in Tobermory, and the only place open was the Princess Hotel. It was 9:00 p.m., and we were lucky to find any place to eat.

When we finished, we had to go back to pick up Bernice's car and then drive back to the B & B. We arrived there at 10:15 p.m. All the lights were off, and it looked closed up for the night. But the door was open, so we snuck in and were in bed and asleep posthaste. It was another memorable day—to say the least.

We had complained about the charges to park in the park until we needed the rescue unit and decided it was certainly money well spent. The charges were partially used for rescuing people who don't know where they are, may be injured, etc. We were so relieved that we had not had an injury other than to our pride. We wondered what the next day would bring. We hadn't hiked very far but had had the experience of a lifetime.

Hike No. 60

June 18, 2009

Thursday again dawned sunny and bright, not a cloud in the sky and just the right temperature to hike. We had had an incredible week, weather-wise. We hoped that this day we would fair much better than we had the day before. We had a very nice breakfast, and having decided to do a small hike and take the rest of the day to rest up for the last hike and the drive home the next day, we got busy and packed up the car.

It was nearly 11:00 a.m. by the time we had parked the car and started out from the Emmett Lake parking area. We decided to do at least part of the hike we had intended to do the previous day before we got going the wrong way. From the parking lot, it was 1 km into the beginning of the Bruce Trail. Arriving at the blazes on the trail, we continued on down to the cobblestone beach and walked a stretch of that and returned back and then started into the bush. Having walked about another kilometer or so, we decided to return. We were tired from the week's events and felt we had done almost 4.5 km that day, so we leisurely drove back to the B & B.

On our way, we detoured to the Crane Lake Side Road, which took us to the end of the hike we had done on Tuesday. It turned out to be 3.3 km from there to our car. So in fact, we had done 18.3km on the Tuesday. No wonder we were so tired that we couldn't wait to get to bed that night. We enjoyed a very pleasant drive while listening to George Gershwin's *Rhapsody in Blue* on the CD player and relaxed fully for the first time in a few days.

Back at the B & B, we had a little nap and then went down to the patio and sat and read our books and enjoyed the sun, the peace and quiet, and a very pleasant afternoon. It was interesting that the weatherman had called for an all-day rain. Those poor weather people made almost as many mistakes as we had been making.

Bernice and I decided to have a 4:00 p.m. cocktail hour. She had a glass of wine and I had a Southern Comfort and ginger ale. We chatted with Sue, our server, and a young couple staying across the hall from us with a cute little baby. It turned out that they were from Cambridge. It is a small world after all.

We enjoyed our dinner, including a delicious homemade pie with a pot of tea, and finally finished around 8:30 p.m. We decided to use the sauna, which really brought on the sleepy eyes, so we returned to our room and were soon fast asleep.

Hike No. 61

June 19, 2009

Friday, June 19, started out very early. We awoke believing it was 8:00 a.m., but it was really only 6:15 a.m. However, we had wanted to get an early start, so indeed we did. I had not been able to find my watch and mentioned it to Sue at breakfast, and she said they would look for it and let me know if they found it. We had another lovely breakfast, one to last us for quite a while. Our cars were already packed, so we thanked Ann and bade farewell to her and her staff. We were excited about starting out the last day of our Bruce Trail odyssey.

It was again a perfect hiking day. At least Mother Nature was being kind to us. We drove to Tobermory, parked Bernice's car, and headed back to the beginning point of our hike. The trail was in the midst of being changed, and not wanting to get lost yet again, we left the car parked where we had intended to start and just walked up Highway 6 toward Tobermory. After about 1 km, we turned down a side road leading toward Georgian Bay and again picked up the trail.

At this point, we really felt like we were back to basics, with rocks, roots, and small inclines and declines. We were skirting the bay but were not able to see the view due to the foliage on the trees. This was a rather unexciting part, except for the fact that we knew each step took us closer to the ultimate end of our journey. We entered the park area and came upon the interpretive center. The center has a high lookout tower. Bernice, on a previous trip, had climbed it, and I did not feel the need to do so at that time. We passed on by and came to the museum. We stopped to take some pictures to commemorate our odyssey.

The trail followed another few blocks to the Northern Terminus and the Cairn overlooking the harbor. I gave the Cairn a great big kiss, delighted that we had finally completed our long, long trail. There is another song title there, "There's a Long, Long Trail Awinding," very old and probably not well-known to many nowadays. However, we had followed the long, long, trail, albeit wandered off at times, missing signs and directions; climbed hills and, in some cases, shinnied down dales; walked over rocks and crawled through crevices; steered clear of bears; and had some scrapes and cuts and some sore muscles and feet. But we had made it to the end. We were ecstatic!

Northern Terminus at Tobermory Got Er Done
June 19 2009—Should be "Dun"

Near the Cairn were some picnic tables, and we were surprised to see the group of hikers from Bernice's church who had also just finished their hike about a half hour prior to our arrival. We congratulated each other, but we were sorry we had missed their champagne toast to mark their completion.

We had had an ice cream cone. What? Bernice doesn't even like ice cream but had promised her friend Audrey (who, many times while at her cottage in Tobermory, had enjoyed ice cream cones) that we would do it, so we did. Our champagne toast came later!

We left Tobermory at about 12:30 p.m., just prior to the docking of the Cheecheemong Ferry from Manitouland Island. The highway south becomes very heavily traveled as the passengers disembark and head back down Highway 6.

Leaving Tobermory, we felt a little deflated now that we have come to the end after all this time, yet we were happy that we had indeed completed our quest. I drove as far as Harriston and stopped at the famous Cedar Rail for a hot dog and a rest before completing the rest of the trip home. As we were driving along, I got a phone call from Ric, informing me that they had called from Cape Chin to say they had found my watch and would mail it to me. That was welcome news.

We arrived at Bernice's around 5:30 p.m. to a welcome-home get-together from Jim and Cathy (Bernice's daughter). Cathy had dropped by on her way from work and brought a bottle of wine to celebrate our completion of the trail. Chris, Cathy's husband, arrived sometime later. Paul (Bernice's son) and daughter-in-law Lynn were on their way from Stratford to join the celebration and arrived around 6:00 p.m. with champagne and a lovely cheese tray and a veggie tray, which we all enjoyed. At one point, Paul was trying to show Lynn how to operate his video camera, and I wondered why he just didn't take the pictures of Bernice and me drinking our champagne himself. He had a purpose in mind. He was busily uncorking another bottle of champagne and managed to catch us totally by surprise and drenched us with the bubbly. It was a great moment to keep for posterity and to commemorate our odyssey.

There were some (we think) who didn't quite believe we could do it! We wondered too, but we kept the faith in spite of all our lost ways and through delays because of sickness, heat, and problems getting together for the time to do it. We persisted, and what a wonderful feeling of accomplishment it was.

After a brief description of our week of trials and tribulations, amid smiles, laughter, and honest-to-goodness disbelief, Bernice's family left for their homes. Jim cooked steaks for our celebration, and we enjoyed a lovely repast and relaxed after our "*that was the week that was*"! I stayed overnight and packed my backpack, pole, boots, water bottles, first aid kit, clothes, sunglasses, etc., for the last time. Nostalgia began to set in. It was the end of a perfectly wonderful adventure, one neither I nor Bernice had ever expected to do. These memories of a great time, with a great friend, would not soon vanish. In fact, they never will!

I can only sum it up with the wish that anyone who wants a great adventure should find a special friend, hike in a very special area like the Bruce Trail, and build a wealth of memories to cherish as long as they live.

I thank Mary so much for sharing some of the trail with us, and Jim and Mary, both of whom drove us so many times and so many kilometers and always managed to somehow find us even when our directions were not quite accurate. Thanks to Ric, who spent many days and nights at home, hoping we would make it back home safe and sound, and to our children who cheered us on over the duration which began in 2001. We sucked ’er up and got ’er dun!

CPSIA information can be obtained at www.ICGtesting.com
Printed in the USA
LVOW061955260413

331153LV00001B/338/P